For myself, for my muse.

CORNERED

Table of Contents

TRILOGY

She fell from the white in a world stained black.

Her clothes were in tatters, and her head reeled.

Above, there was a three-cornered skylight.

"Am I myself as I was, or someone I will become?"

Cornered: Overgrown Garden

Yesterday, I forgot to trim the roses. Clusters of brush lay as stark greens over sandy grit, which have their branches and stems mixed into the typical reddish-brown earth. I hadn't noticed they'd grown—everything's grown, really, but the roses are standouts. If I'd been paying attention, I'd have noticed sooner. Their thorny stems are motionless, ever-threatening, a contrast to their blushing blossoms. Blossoms now dwarfing my hands.

...They've been growing too much.

Soil pools between my toes, the driest pieces falling off as I wander back to the trail of stepping stones. Daylight shines through the greenery. The sun—I've never observed it, but it seemed to be sunlike—relieves a cold rush I'd suffered a second before, even as I'm struck by another. I hug both arms, rubbing the sides while I'm walking along. Shade hangs overhead from towering ferns and bushes—not once has a breeze rushed through, betraying the often-chilled air seeping into the atmosphere. I stroll onto the smooth stones, hopping across them like some banal child. At least it isn't more dirt.

I pause. Third step from the last, seventeenth from the cabin.

Maybe I wouldn't have missed pruning if I'd known where my tools went. Though in reality, they were never *my* tools. They could've been taken for cleaning. Or are they being replaced? I can't be certain. For the length of time I've lived in this place, I haven't been awake to watch things change.

Believe me, I've tried holding my eyelids open. It's impossible. The calming lavender aroma persists no matter how many I find and tear from their roots—there must be more of them. Further in, or further *out.* Then again, whenever I destroy a few plants, several grow back in their place the following morning. This is unheard of. And every time the absurdity catches up with me, I stop myself, because it'll do no good. Panicking is unreasonable, and it invites things I can't comprehend.

What if another of those dolls shows up?

Forward, forward. Come on, then. I count down the steps, plodding over the stones. Repeated, simulated birdsong chirps mindlessly above, still signaling morning. Slowing pace, I breathe in the clean air.

That's the funny thing: wherever I am, it's livable. I'm allowed a small cabin to eat and sleep in—almost there, I've just trod across the tenth stone—and I never go without. A shiver runs between my legs. Well, maybe I *am* missing a bit of vital clothing. Underwear's out to dry, and I have exactly one outfit to go with it. Just a plain, cottony smock barely covering anything below, ending before the middle of my thighs. Laundry day isn't a chore, but hardly a silver lining. I pull the dress down by its rim, studying a fraying hem that refuses to be stretched; it slides up again. *Off-white* lining.

I don't like airy clothing. Feels like it could disappear any second. Although I haven't met another person, to think if I'd be left wearing this, speaking with someone…how mortifying. Though I'm not sure I've ever been so modest at home. On my own, however, I'd be the one deciding to dress or undress, not the unknown powers-which-might-be. I'd also have more clothes. The towels are too small, though I also can't cover myself with the bedsheets—they'd get dirty outside.

There's an idea I haven't tried: sewing more dresses from the bedsheets. Why didn't I—I should've thought of it sooner! If I hadn't been so busy…

No, enough planning. How am I going to find time to cut the blankets, sew a dress—how would I make a needle? What if I hurt myself? This is stupid, I'm stupid. Why am I embarrassed to *hypothetically* encounter someone? No one is around. Plants are around, but I can't withstand cutting them for long; if I don't clip their branches, I can only travel so deep into those limbs, as far as walking goes. Body's useless, like I've become the first living gelatin. All because I'm here.

Whispering slithers among the trees, voices I both recognize and refuse. I'm sure I can't go back home. Follow the plan; this is home now. It'd be best to think it had always been. Or else I won't be able to smile.

A slip into the dirt nicks my heel, pulling me from a muddled mind. Wincing, I brush off the earth, setting on the path again—here lies the remainder of it.

Grayish patio tiles begin where the ivory stepping stones end, and standing above it all, the log cabin stands, a lighthouse within a fog of foliage. Yet always dark. While I'm gone, the lights turn off and stay off. My hand runs over a wooden armchair as I walk across the porch, letting fingers hover to the cabin's outer wall. Gliding through the grooves in its natural bark, unlike the stripped surface inside. Yes, I'm going in now. Right.

I take the door handle, curling a fist over the cool, burnished iron. It clicks with the press of my thumb.

The door pushes smoothly. I've oiled the hinges some days ago; I correct them at the slightest squeak, an easier task compared to pruning plants. Not much maintenance for the cabin otherwise. Holding the door ajar, I edge forward. Dim. Quiet, for now. Negative, shadowing space mingles with sections of light. Ornate metal adorns a window resting above the kitchenette—the fancy frame is, fittingly, floral in nature.

Ah, now the door's wide open. But I haven't stepped inside. I peer as far as I can, watching the modest bedspread. Elegantly dressed toys lean against each other on the nearby shelf. Although the bedside window is a replica of the kitchen's, it's missing half the swirled decoration on its sill. My palms sweat.

I enter the cabin.

With both feet on its parquet flooring, everything springs to light. A lamp overhead illuminates the one-room lodge. On the shelf, two dolls smile back unwittingly, their frilly, wrinkled dresses a matching pink and white, and white and pink. I don't turn from them to shut the door. My back nudges it closed.

"Welcome home, Miss Margot!" a sociable man announces.

The source, humming to himself, crawls from under the bed, four spindled legs supporting his black sphere of a body. It circles the mattress, facing a circular screen toward me—the cartoonish, virtual eyes grin.

"Good morning!" his voice prompts a bluish line on-screen, which ripples with the peaks and lows of his tone; "Did you enjoy your walk?"

I shuffle to the kitchen sink, revisiting a forgotten dish. White marred by greasy leftovers. Stealing a sponge from its resting place, I grab the plate and start scrubbing.

"Did you enjoy your walk?" the robot echoes. The exact inflection as before—questioning at the end, eagerly lifting. Not quite natural.

"Yes." I scrape at a persistent speck. "I enjoyed it."

He processes plain remarks in a half second.

"That's wonderful!" he says while scaling the counter, a subtle whir of his innards conveying a struggle. The polymer legs play against varnished wood like fingernails. Only when reaching the top do the mechanical sounds wane, his body just within peripheral sight.

I swipe the last crumb free and wash it down the sink.

"I'm so happy you're happy!"

Impossible. I smile anyway, ensuring his eye notices.

His fake eyes grin again on-screen. The robot buzzes as he does a little dance back and forth, a wobble lasting two seconds—without music, he stops shortly after.

"SPIKE, tell me the time," I request. He's very good at this one.

Without a breath passing, he displays it and says, "The time is currently eight fourteen."

That'll quiet him a bit. While the *8:14* is plastered on his face, I twist the knob on the sink. Left, for hot water.

Though it first rushes out somewhat cold, the water heats soon enough, and I run the plate under the stream. Soap—I knew I forgot something. I grab the bottle and squirt a drop onto the dish.

SPIKE continues acting like a clock.

I wield the sponge, putting my nervousness to work. Lather collects under the flow of water.

Fourteen hours to go. Fourteen hours of time that isn't free. Ignoring SPIKE makes him comment on things more frequently, my punishment being his constant reminders; reminders become discipline if I'm not careful, and they're the only case where he can move wherever he wants. SPIKE won't leave the cabin if I do things right. He's just a machine, and machines are wired to act predictably.

I shiver. People don't perform the same, myself included. Order can only keep machines at ease. SPIKE's companionship barely passes for a facsimile of humanity, yet it tricks the mind, it appeals to the lowest bar. I usually fend off the discomfort of knowing this, but I'm starting to crack.

Today marks a week since I've counted the days, more or less feeling like months. SPIKE gives hours, not dates, and he hasn't been helpful since. Assisting the way *he* wants: with ideas he's programmed to offer.

You'd think your own room would be the most private place you have, but no. Try having a robot watching everything you do—fake smiles, fake interest, very real tasks I can't leave to rot. I'm never bored; there's no peace. Under his regime, those giant plants start looking friendlier by the day. I guess the ferns and bushes might feel like they're watching at times, but...but when I cry or scream around them, they brush against me. They're strangely soothing.

But if I'm distressed around SPIKE, I wake up to an emotional support doll on my pillow.

My hands are wrinkling. I set the sponge aside, plate and upper arms still drenched in water. The shelf catches the corner of my eye.

They haven't moved, have they? No, no. Both are sitting—wait, they're looking this way. I turn off the faucet.

Another glance over. A pair of porcelain faces offer their perpetual smiles, bodies unmoving. Their heads shift.

I shudder and just nearly scream—a soft, prickling sense brings attention to SPIKE, whose front legs are now resting on my forearm.

"Can we do something else, Margot?" he pleads, looking up at me. "Can we, can we?"

From the shelf, one of the two dolls cries out, "Read us a story!"

The other gradually stands. "Read to us, SPIKE!"

They're impossible to tell apart on voice alone since they're the same model of toy, and they even wear similar gowns. In fact, despite being quite a flimsy marker, their dresses are the sole reason I can name them. A sixth sense of sorts had given me the idea to write their names on their legs as well. The dolls can only stand and sit, but I like to take precautions. I've already mistaken them once before.

SPIKE leaves my arm to jump from the counter, bracing on the hardwood once he lands. Before rushing off, he halts not far from my feet, deferring again, "Why don't you pick out a story for us, Margot? I can read anything with lots of words."

Yves, dressed in white and pink, continues standing. She stares.

The third pair of hollow eyes are Alice's, the doll in pink and white.

I first leave the dish—I've been clutching it for comfort—on the drying rack, then return to the audience three. Each is patient, though I have plans already. Reading will waste time. Besides, we don't have more than—

"Come on, Margot! Let's sit over here," SPIKE starts, scuttling to the bed impatiently. "It'll be fun to read together."

Fidgeting, I stall by turning around, grabbing for a hand towel. Can't hold paper with wet hands, after all. The weight of their fake eyes presses into my back, evoking the same, familiar tension. As if I've shattered a glass in a crowded restaurant.

It's going to be the poem again. I hate it, I hate it so, so much. SPIKE knows when I'm late or haven't eaten, but he can't understand a question like "Can I have more books?" He holds idle conversations until I ask for things, then he's suddenly a dumb robot with no answers. And I know what he's doing now. This is to keep me busy—everything is to keep busy, keep occupied. Stay in, don't leave.

He'll be in for a surprise later.

Fake, happy expressions—robots are too calculated for honesty. It's only fair I return the favor. I spin back to the three toys, smiling dumbly, and bathe in hopeful thoughts. SPIKE's legs are pressed close to his round form. Snug on the blanket, he wiggles, until he doesn't. Feigned comfort.

The dolls flank either side of him. Yves is the one sitting this time, knees locked, perpetually bent arms frozen at her navel. Alice wobbles, the bed too soft for her to hold still.

I plunk onto the mattress.

"Whoa!" Alice says her line while toppling onto her back. She shifts her arms and head, the motion whirring and clicking. Pushing herself up, Alice returns to a sitting position, remarking, "Teehee, whoopsie. I fell!"

Spiteful bliss creeps into another smile of mine. I'm glad SPIKE can't tell the difference. Oh, Alice! If I had one of you as a child, I would've never gotten enough. I'm absolutely losing my mind. I'd knock her over again now, but the little joys aren't worth prolonging this. The sooner I read, the sooner I'm granted a sliver of freedom. A human euphoria ravaging all sanity: *freedom.*

"SPIKE, what time is it?" I ask.

"The time is currently eight twenty-one, Miss Margot." He displays the number proudly.

Thirteen hours, thirty-nine minutes. I bend down, grabbing the book from under the bed, and then lay it on my lap. Opening it, I turn it over to show to the robot's camera eye.

"SPIKE, read this," I declare loud and clear.

He crawls on Alice's dress, steadying himself to scan the pages.

"It looks like you want me to read: *The Hunting of the Snark* by Lewis Carroll. Is that correct?" he says.

"Yes."

I don't want him to, I just don't have a choice.

SPIKE's face gets replaced by an hourglass, with digital sand dropping to its empty side, turning once it fills. One...four, five...it'll be ten seconds, I think. Six, seven, eight—at nine, his fake eyes blink open. Almost ten.

"Okay!" He straightens, nodding his body. "Get comfortable, and when you're ready, tell me to read. We are currently on line—"

"Read page one."

SPIKE pauses once more.

"Page one," he says after two seconds. *"Fit the First. The Landing."*

***

"Your turn, Miss Margot!"

It isn't. We're done. I've finished the final set of lines, the *Fit* is over, gone and gone. Nonsense gives me rashes. If I'm trapped for a second *Fit*, I'm throwing a tantrum. Why isn't he asking to take a break?

SPIKE, lingering on his own line, remains perfectly immobile.

"I like this story," comments Alice.

"I like this story," another aside echoes from Yves. They're the same model of doll, after all.

Five seconds pass before I'm able to answer.

"Have you lost your place? If you have, I will repeat the last passage," chimes SPIKE. "If not, I will resume where you've left off and switch to auto-reading mode. Would you like me to—"

"Pause!" I demand.

SPIKE's screen flickers. "Sorry," he says, "I don't understand what you mean. Could you—"

"Stop!" I shout.

"Sorry, I don't understand—"

Damn machine. Entertaining him is useless. I jump to my feet, escaping the mattress and its inhuman guards. Warm as the carpeting is, the floorboards I reach are not, their chill turning a walk to an uneven skip. Luckily, the cabin is very small. Light—real or not—and sunbaked earth are steps away.

I take hold of the door's handle.

"SPIKE," I call as I open it, "I am going to check the laundry."

"You wish to complete the following chore: laun—"

Door goes shut, and I trap the unmagical eight-ball in the cabin. Simple. A curve around the porch, a hop into the dirt—a swivel as I clear the corner in less than a minute. Less than the time it takes for SPIKE to answer something, maybe. As quickly as I stop behind the cabin, I reach out and pinch both undergarments off the clothesline, which remains attached to the roof's edge. The line nearly twangs.

With no dryer, air is the best I have to keep these scarce clothes mildly less soggy; the top slips on easily, though it isn't a real bra. A cropped shirt, I think—the underwear's bottoms are at least well-fitted. By now I've thrown the off-white dress into a washing tub, as always, because there is no washer either. The important plumbing is within the cabin instead: sink, shower, and the smallest toilet I'd ever seen. Everything is claustrophobic inside, the bathroom so terribly cramped I've almost considered using the garden. I prefer the fresh outdoors. Oversized plants and all.

The faucet squeaks, water trickling out of the backyard hose— in barely a *yard,* as the flora obscures the height of an untainted glass. Steps from the cabin, I aim the hose above a small firepit. There, a metal bucket dangles on an iron hook, soldered to a similarly iron pillar, which had been rooted into the earth. By whoever put the cabin here, I suppose.

While filling the hefty bucket, the vines and bushes watch me from their perch on the glass. I toddle forward, backward. Heels up, then down. Glass walls...this place is a round, clear prison of glass. Some odd mix between a snow globe (the cabin) and terrarium (everything else), though giant enough that I would grow tired running from end-to-end. The creeping plants seem to always stop halfway to the top of the sphere. Just like me, they can't get out.

Water soaks only a little dirt before I whip the hose back to the patio, where the stream splatters against stone. *Squeak.* Off, you hose. There.

But you see, as down-to-earth as this laundry method is, I'm always met with the anomaly of technology. I sit beside the firepit. On one of the circle's fake, inlaid rocks, I push a protruding button made to blend into its pattern. A flame springs to life.

The metal bucket warms—so does the water. A rag is still lounging below the iron pillar, but it doesn't matter if it's dirty. It isn't for cleaning things: I use it to shield my hands from the heated bucket. Why bother? I ask myself each day I do the laundry, really. The answers never change. *Boiling water won't work, it hurts. And it doesn't get rid of him.*

SPIKE had returned the day after I'd attempted to drown him as if nothing ever happened. I bought time when I'd done it (short-circuiting the body), gaining precious hours without a robot occupying any, but ever since, I've been dragged around. Waking, eating, reading, eating, gardening, music-listening, *eating,* sleeping. Every day, sometimes in a varied order. But the meals became strict after the drowning.

Delicate shudders run through a forearm; nightly curfew is another unspoken danger—SPIKE would scold before, a time ago, but he'd welcome me inside. I'd often fall asleep with the calming scents from the flowering plants. Then came the night he found me again, his lenience dropped. I...I need to prevent that.

Untamed vines hug the glass along with the topiary border. Most plants here are thorny or itchy—or too weak to hold a person. There are no trees, only the tallest shrubs and thickest bushes for roses, azaleas, and the occasional blueberries. I don't trust myself enough to eat from them. Poisoning is as slow and excruciating as suffering burns; I have no other way out.

At least if I escape, I can find out where I am. Far above the wall, following the flawless barrier, it's possible to make out a place where the glare doesn't quite reflect off anything. A circle. An *opening*, like an honest to God terrarium. I don't care how high it is!

That's where I'm going when—

Burbling sounds reach my ears, then a click. The fire's gone.

Time really isn't the same anymore; I'm not even sure if I know what *anymore* used to be.

The odd firepit snuffs out once the water boils, on cue, in three minutes. Which produces what I need to wash a singular cloth. I jump to my feet to grab the tub first, and then tuck the washboard beside it under an arm. With a moment or more—to let the bucket cool slightly below scalding—I pour the water into the tub.

Set down the washboard, place the dress across its ridges.

I let a deep breath drive might into my arms.

***

Where did I leave it? Rummaging through soil and rock, I grab handfuls at a time, teeth holding my bottom lip under the other. First the tools gone, then the metal hook—I thought SPIKE was unconscious when I'd made it. I broke him—boiled him—he shouldn't have been aware. He wasn't meant to see or hear. Could he still process movement? Record me?

What in *God's name* is that robot?

I can't even find the twine. It took hours upon hours to fashion rope from the rose stems; to shave down the thorns; to weave them together; to pull them taut and test their strength against my thin frame. Climbing onto the cabin roof would've been the first test—I don't have the rope now. I can't do it.

Noontide deepens all around, light waning from the unknown sun. I feel into the dirt. Impossible for anyone to find it. The robots don't ignore their programmed instinct, and plants can't move. A rough, fragile thing brushes up against my shoulder.

I'm leaning into the bushes. Maybe they grew over the original spot where I'd buried my grappling hook; maybe they sprouted, like the unnatural things they are. I dig until the roots scrape my fingernails.

The world's light turns pitch black.

I haven't been out long—it was noon a minute ago. What time is it? I don't know what time it is. I don't know the time!

Crawling further, the pathetic struggle yields only the remnants of nature. No, there it is! I swipe through more dirt. The clumps fall back into the rest along with my tired hands, and the dogged pursuit drags me forward. I claw at the visions of rope as the earth clogs my skinned elbows and knees. Something shines ahead. A glare. Metal? *The hook?*

I lunge over to it—my head thuds against a cold, solid wall. Brow throbbing in the aftermath, I watch as the sparks flicker on the surface. Glass. I'm at the edge of the terrarium.

"The time is currently past nineteen by three minutes."

SPIKE had followed me out.

"Please return to the cabin."

I pound the glass, screaming frustration until it fogs over—it's cold. There's no sun anymore. I'm freezing; I hadn't finished drying the laundry because I left to find the hook. And rope. I should've waited for tomorrow—I should've been dressed for this.

But instead, my skin is left unprotected. Would it have mattered? Wishful thinking—how can I believe a dress could've helped me?

"How the mind rationalizes when it's all over."

I glance to SPIKE's voice, and I find the blackened silhouettes empty. Fronds rustle from there; a hum cuts through the growth. Everything adjusts as I blink the obscurity away.

A flash throws my gaze sideways. Guttural clicking and crackling fulminates with the tempo of those blinding flickers. In stumbling back, I catch a shade between the arcs—SPIKE's figure darts forward.

My chest erupts with an air of flight, puffing out as I launch like a marathon runner, pain swelling under my breast—there's nowhere to go. My palm guides me onward when the sprint overtakes every thought, every action. My fingertips, at the end of it all, inform that I'm still treading near the wall. Freezing glass. Rock underfoot tearing at rough skin, thorns and branches whipping from ankle to hip.

My toes snag at a root I couldn't have seen. I lurch forward.

Thump.

The earth smears into my pores.

Light flashes from behind—shadows come and go. I force an arm out to find the ground, to somehow drag to my feet again.

SPIKE crawls onto an ankle.

"No!" I shriek, I yell and shake him off; "Stay—stay away from— no, *no!* God, *please!*"

Prongs sink into my calf. A shockwave fires through every vein; as quick as it comes on, my body surrenders itself. The crackling jolts into my ears. Limbs fall neither cold nor hot—they're deadened, I can't move them. Spasms clench every muscle with a pain I'd never wanted to feel again. I can't move.

SPIKE's voice sizzles and cuts through:

"Please re—to the, ca—"

Another set of prongs jam into a thigh—I barely feel SPIKE. And it starts over. Muscles contracting in further, renewed jolts. Nerves quaking, they refuse to relay anything but surges of pain, and I kiss the ground without restraint.

"Plea—re-turn to—cabin."

I *can't,* you bastard!

"SPIKE!" I try to scream—my lower jaw raps against the upper half.

"Please return—cabin—to—please."

My mouth seizes.

The robot bites harder. *More electricity.*

My heart beats as wild as the clacking from behind; the sound dulls in what must be insufferable hours, a writhing sense spurring more spasms, its signal in paradox with the body I can't control.

I can't feel my throat—I don't know how to breathe. Ovules arranged in a web of lights rise from beyond the glass. The hive stares back with reflections of faces. All my own face, and uncountable, their features petrified. A spotlight shines from somewhere, beaming directly into both eyes. Then at mine.

Home. I've got to go home ...

I choke and spit onto the ground.

The lights ...

My mind is the last to go.

***

A cute little ball of energy scurries onto the bedsheets, displaying a black screen with pinkish eyes. And a few pixels reserved for fake blush.

Reaching to its head—or, I guess the top of its body—I give it a tap. The machine jostles. It blinks on-screen.

"Good morning!" Her voice runs much silkier than I expect. No staccato or static.

... her voice?

"You're a talking robot, then," I remark, patting the unliving creature once more.

She awkwardly holds still.

"Who are you?" I whisper.

Humming accompanies a tip of her body. She lifts herself with four legs, which appear segmented like an insect—odd that she only has four. Six or eight would seem appropriate, but maybe she doesn't need more.

"New user number designated *380021*. Hello, world. Please repeat your name slowly," she says.

I'm not sure if I should, but ...

"Mar-got." I sound the syllables as clearly as possible.

The robot pauses to show me an hourglass on its face—oh, she's processing it! I see.

"From the database, *Margot* is registered under *female baby names*," recites the object, "Your name will be displayed on-screen now"—it shows *MARGOT* scrolling across in neon pink—"is this correct?"

"Y-yes." I marvel at my reflection in the clean, ivory surface, noticing a smudge from where I'd touched the polished body. Oh, dear. That's going to bother me.

As I consider buffing out the blemish, I realize I'm wearing an off-white dress, and around me are bedsheets matching a lighter rose; beyond the mattress lies the rest of the room, stealing a moment's breath. It's wonderful. A log cabin with a kitchen on one side—parallel to the bed I'm in—and windows without curtains on both.

"Look at *this*," I mutter aloud, feeling the silvery decoration that frames the nearest window. A spiral adornment sits on either half, like vines patterned with leaves, though one of them is broken. The rough edge pokes my fingertip—I recoil, luckily unhurt. Did someone break it?

"All set!"

I flit back to the robot. Her body vibrates as if she's a dog shaking off bathwater, quivering before she crawls backward. She nods at me.

"Welcome, Miss Margot. I am your Smart-Pal Infused Kinetic Exoskeleton!" she says. A pink line wobbles and settles on her face, following the voice. "But you may call me SPIKE."

Forcing the shears to work takes all the force I have, but it's the best way to trim the rose bushes. SPIKE had assigned me the task of gardening. In a huge, sprawling mass of plants, might I add. It kills time and sweats out my worries, so I don't have many complaints.

Although, I'd like to learn where this place is. Logically speaking, if I remember my first name, I wasn't born here. Was I? I'm definitely a *human*—and I know what *human* means. Math, a bit of history, understanding the nature of...nature. I'm no green thumb, but SPIKE came with a pamphlet for herself, and I'd learned how to ask her about the plants.

These roses are much larger than my head, so I'd assumed they needed special care to survive. Not so. In fact, they need little tending aside from clearing away overgrown stems. Same as the other plants; whether fern, bush, grass, or flower, every one of them just requires a trim. At first, I'd wondered why—a few days in and I have my answer: the plants grow overnight.

I shear off another stem. Two roses plummet along with their thorny necks, wrinkling under the crisp air. Petals softly glide down and land at my feet. Leaves pile beneath the bush.

Grow is almost an understatement. The plants sprout faster than weeds, and I swear, whenever I walk around, they emerge from their ground to grab my heels. I haven't seen another person around, but at least I have these beautiful flowers to keep me company.

Inside, I have SPIKE. Outside? Fresher scents and more flourishing sights than I could've ever dreamed of. This aroma—I think it's lavender. Small florets along the various natural paths; larger clusters hiding among the taller grasses; and yes, I'm even strolling between them whenever I shuffle next to the topiaries. No people...ah, but it's so peaceful! I can get used to this.

Their heaviness taking a toll, I discard the giant shears and sit down beside them. Tugging at my soaked collar reminds me I'll have to launder it soon—maybe this afternoon—if I don't want to feel disgusting. Phew. Can gardening be exercise? It sure feels like it.

A whitish sunlight shines over the world, only accentuating the heat. It's both familiar and unfamiliar. It can't be *the* Sun. I don't see a horizon, just more fog in the distant gray. Where the plants are the shortest, the color is easier to pick out.

I frame the stepping stones with my fingers; the cabin just above it; plant life everywhere else; and a strange figure disturbing the green. A brownish cascade like a pile of deadened grass, but so obscured by the overgrowth, I must've missed the irregular thing during the walk. I'd pranced from stone to stone while counting them, all twenty-one; my remaining awareness tried to memorize landmarks. The memory of the path would keep me from drowning in vegetation. Far more important than spotting weird, remote plants.

But, I *am* a gardener. If that's a dead plant, I should dig it up.

I fish around the toolbox (I forgot I'd brought it, really), equipping both a machete and small, yet sturdy spade. The larger shovel is back at the cabin, and I don't want to loiter. What sort of plant could look like burnt straw? A stout palm tree? No, I haven't seen any trees...this may be the first. All the reason to investigate before sundown.

Once I finish burying the plant clippings, I start hacking my way through the plants and trekking in the oddity's direction. At times I lose sight of it—the ferns whip into my face, and the bushes scratch my legs—but it gets closer the more I strive onward, never taking more than a glance away.

I clutch the spade, swinging the machete in front. Fronds and branches fly apart. Though a few twigs nick my forehead, the march doesn't stop; I heave in and out to power every stride.

"What?"

Lips parted, I halt at a clearing of dirt. I drop the spade; I drop the machete. A panted, unintelligible word falls from the same mouth that once admired the garden.

I step over to the figure. Disheveled strands conceal where the breasts had been left bare, a ripped cloth falling from a pair of sunken shoulders. I look the body up and down. Down and up.

An uncanny head gazes forward, mouth agape—a human filled to its eye sockets. Infested with weeds and wrung out by vines, and legs apart like a skinned teddy bear on a shelf. But with no shelf, the form is left in the dirt, sores trailing up its ankles, over knees and thighs, ferns growing between—

Dryness heaves from my throat; I have nothing to throw up and out. Bile festers within those walls, stomach burning. No better than a heart trembling too much for me to bear. *Get out of here! Leave, leave!* It tells me to move using every physical burden it can, but cruelly buckles my shaking legs. What do you want from me? To leave, isn't that right? The urge of flight is swept behind an overpowering fright, taking strength with it. I can't go. I can't—not like this!

Collapsed into the earth; digging fingers into the soil; and ignoring the pain of it pooling under my nails, I lift my head to suck in the stale air. I hold it in. Despite its disgusting flavor, tinged with the metal and grime of recent decay. I push the breath through my mouth. And again—limbs still quivering as struggle like some dying animal—I take more careful inhales. Pausing, fighting a weak chill. Exhaling. *I'm going to die. I'm dying here.*

No, you're not, you're not.

Though tears blot out half the vision, I catch the most peculiar detail on the corpse in front of me. I don't know why—I recognize it. Is she...?

A ladybug crawls from the left eye socket, rustling the feathery leaves.

I'm going to—

I bite down into my tongue. It hurts and distracts enough, shooting feeling through once deadened limbs, giving me a push to my feet; I run for my own life, from death, straight toward home.

***

"SPIKE, SPIKE!"

I bash the door open wailing for the companion, snuffling back the streaming tears and snot.

"SPIKE!"

Hobbling—ankle sprained and bruising—I'm able to reach the bed, but the last of my energy depletes while wrenching the sheets off. I collapse on the mattress, gulping. Gasping. Nobody should have to feel their heart squeeze itself to near-death.

I wheeze into a pillow. "SPIKE."

Goosebumps scramble up my arm—I pull it away. The robot pauses at the edge of the bed, its pixelated smile still on-screen. A red light shines into my forehead.

"Miss Margot, your body temperature is too high."

Her honeyed words soothe as much as her permanent smile. Coincidentally, the expression changes, a cartoonish pout replacing her innocent mirth.

"You may have a fever," she says, "please wait here."

"No, SPIKE," I whimper too quietly.

Tiny, metallic arms emerge from hidden sockets on her body, their rubber claws like open hands; she hurries across the floor, scaling various drawers and hopping up to the kitchen sink.

She grabs the hand towel. Water flushes from the faucet, seeping into the thick cloth.

"Someone's out there," I ramble aloud. My arms tremble if I even think to start moving again. "There's a body out there. I saw a body, SPIKE."

The robot returns holding a plate, where the wet towel is safely apart from her machinery. SPIKE begins to whirr—she drops the cold compress on my forehead.

"SPIKE!" I yell.

She freezes.

"SPIKE, there is a *dead* body," I say, snatching the towel and throwing it off the bed. "I found a body in the garden!"

Her form holds in place.

What am I doing? This isn't a person; she can't help me. But nobody can, anyway—I'm alone, I'm the only woman alive in the garden. I gulp once more, a lump wedged where I can't swallow. I'm still able to inhale, but it trembles, rattling whenever I exhale.

"Lead me to the site."

Her arms retract; SPIKE leaps backward. All four legs patter against the floor, adjusting the spherical body, as her innards drone louder—this cabin is silent save for the sound, as if we're both able to breathe. She stares at me with a blank screen.

I push up and onto an elbow.

"Please, lead me to it, Margot," says SPIKE. "I will follow."

"You can talk to me?" I sit upright, only to slouch into my knees. "You're really talking to me? Am I crazy?"

"Margot." The robot climbs to my shoulders. "Lead me to where you found it."

"I'm having a conversation. There's no way—you—a sentient robot can't exist, I'm just—I'm scared." I stand up. "SPIKE, what's going to happen to me?"

"Please walk outside."

"Where am I? This isn't a paradise. I'm not already dead—I've bled on the gardening tools before, I know I can be cut. I'm alive."

The robot delicately prods my neck with one of its limbs. "Please," she says, "walk outside of the cabin."

I don't have the will to talk anymore. Both feet, one after the other, step across the floor until I manage to end at the welcome mat.

When I leave, my bearings on the place falter. Except for remembering the body and where I'd discovered it: must be the west of where I'm facing. It was east from the other end. Which makes it west here.

"Margot, please show me—"

I break into a staggering jog, no longer heeding the pain at my ankle. Ignoring the robot—for the entire journey—I force an unwilling body into the bushes, grazing against the overgrowth while I retread a mental path. Along the crumbling earth, once I skid a heel across a flatter patch, and twice I rip ferns from their stems in a blind frenzy. Tears gather under my eyes.

"There…" I point as I'm running.

SPIKE crawls atop my head.

Though I stop myself, I hold the trembling gesture. Words don't seem to come out—I fight to catch my breath.

"Step closer," SPIKE instructs.

Toward the body? "No…I-I don't want to."

"I must be within three feet to examine—"

"Alright! I'll go," I shout, reluctantly approaching the corpse. And kneeling in front of its overtaken skull. The plants curl into themselves. A person—she was a person, but now…"Is this close enough?"

"Yes."

SPIKE returns to a shoulder, perching there as she points her screen—the camera at its topmost point—at the dead woman.

My eyes are closed. If I look at it again, I'll vomit.

A forceful buzz hits under an ear; something snaps.

"Wh—?" I start.

Something bites. Lightning, like a divine strike rupturing my body—the fangs sink deeper. I limply topple over, smashing into a jutting rock. I shriek louder than ever before, throat tearing itself apart. Pain ripples out from my shoulder. Convulsions pin me to the earth, and yet, I can't move a thing.

Garbled clicking repeats from the robot's speakers. A hiss.

SPIKE, I mouth to her, but she crawls over the body, still formulating some verbal jargon no human has ever spoken. A glitch? A bug?

A headache steals my voice for good. I can only scream and drool into the dirt, watching as the artificial intelligence abandons me.

Smaller vines wrap around a finger—where I can see them. Every limb is dead, disobedient.

"SPIKE!"

The nauseating shriek rips the last of my strength away.

"It's a shame," the robot says from afar. It wants me to hear. "I'd just gotten another one."

A calming, persistent odor scorches a final breath, setting the lungs alight. Roots spring from the ground. They lunge at my face; they burrow through every orifice. I no longer scream, nor struggle.

And I choke till death on iron and lavender.

Cornered: Outer Galaxy

Irregular flares glimmer across the void of space, far from my location, before they fizzle into the obsidian. Familiar as the occurrence may be, I cannot be certain of its source. I haven't finished patrolling yet—I'll leave the plan in my mental queue.

Newer stars are the least ripe, you see. I could never rationalize enduring their taste, because they have none to speak of, at best a melting droplet under the tongue. Such a disappointment to travel so far, only for the reddish orb to be no wider than my corpulent neck. Which sheds light on my current predicament: I've found another immature star.

Though the journey left me famished, I don't enjoy the idea of accepting an unripe red. Not again. Both major eyestalks survey the sides; the front pair spots a distant glow. I hunch my neck toward its favorable hue. White, abated stars are *more* than promising. They're the finest we could ask for.

Hurtling into its light, I bring both arms to my sides, legs pressing together as my form assimilates to a narrower position, sticking without melding. I mimic the flow of the tail, or perhaps it mimics the body—altogether I swivel like the passing nebulae. Violets cast over my left, scarlet clouds illuminating the right. Their scent lessens our appetite. Foul, degrading into burnt hairs. O! To be a lower being and have an ignorance of heavenly smell! If I could die, then I'd rather be reborn as one.

Everywhere is another realm, but none were like the Earthen planet. Their sun isn't ripe yet; it wasn't then, either. I passed it as I would any other galaxy, to steer away from planets, and yet I'd been drawn to an odd distortion. Voices. Billions of voices, speaking in numerous tongues. In a fit of burgeoning curiosity, I had camouflaged my sizeable figure (in comparison to theirs, as I am quite normal for my kind), thereafter inserting my psyche into a bystander. He had no sense of me. So, I put myself to the task of learning languages.

Over years in their times, my studious vacation became a source of enjoyment I'd never fathomed—exceeding the most mouthwatering stars, though my only purpose had ever been to feed. We breathe in the stars, and we replenish energy. Then by chance we might find another to breed. But these creatures, the Humanity, had more desires for no apparent purpose. Some would kick objects around for sport—in fact many sports were simply games with kicking or throwing—and others took to scholarly, reclusive occupations. Occupation, yes. A means for acquiring resources, much like our journey across the universe. Particular occupations ascribe themselves duties related to the very space I inhabit. Funniest of all is their visual spectrum—to think the color I perceive is considered falsehood, from the Humanity perspective. All this because they spend so much time collecting information.

Unknown is foreign to them—how admirable. Could you believe their meticulous research? You must have some idea, being one of them yourself. Unless, you aren't. That would be strange. If you were one of mine, did you happen to learn from the Earthen peoples as well?

"That's a silly idea," you might tell me. It is. As silly as we are, who eat the dying stars, and yet living things such as you are poisons to us. Perhaps that is why the—ah, there's no trouble arrogating your words, is there?—well, those I would call the Eaters are nigh extinct.

Eaters...those who once ate the planets. We've outlived them, and we still find room to—

"Running somewhere, are you?"

Given that I'm nearing the end of my territory, the voice must belong to—I hope it doesn't belong to another. It's a tad gravelly, a throaty bass prompting my instinct. If the white luminance is outside my current patrol, I'll have to fight for it.

A weightier star draws my attention. For a vantage point, it'll do. I weave around the snaking trails dispersed by a sprawling nebula, ascending perpendicular to the shifty silhouette. If I have to fight, I simply can't go without sustenance.

"Lovely selection you've got there," says the distant Breather.

Although he may be floating about the cluster of immature stars, he's finally close enough to discern, both in body and face. What a face it is! The essence of the opposite sex is a stronger, flatter skull—the presence of a solid skull at all is an evidence marking his masculinity. Teeth pointed as his, similarly, are absent from the feminine mouth. I have no use for them, as I wouldn't be fighting another male. Had he fought for his territory?

Xiphoid bones trail from his wrists to wide, but svelte shoulders. Smaller at his neck, they lead above his cheeks, stopping below the holes of his ears and nostrils. None are missing. So, he's claimed this spot without usurping another of ours, it seems. Or he may carry such skill and intimidation, he drives his opponents off before he can bare those incisors. Should I ask? I'm a bit nervous. He's too mysterious, and I've never met a male Breather before.

"You intend to keep it to yourself?" He points a claw.

"Why, no," I hover above the orangish giant—I've never shared a star before, either. "But if you earned your boundaries through pacifism, I'll have you know I subdued at least *two* others for mine. What say you of yours?"

"Eleven," his voice lingers on its sound; "I felled eleven thousand."

And yet he has no scars. "I've no reason to believe you."

Retracting his claws, he then flexes his spikes, turning to display a brawny shoulder blade. Glowing, unhealed scrapes cover his back, lines of cuts on either side near the spine. Likewise, the segments of his tails bear notches from tooth and claw. But the freshest wounds must be where I'd started: his shoulders. He'd played with cowards.

"Eleven thousand cowards," I mutter through him.

"Are you impressed?" He pivots his face on that shorter, but sturdier neck of his.

Lights are precious. I shouldn't share. I shouldn't.

"Or, perhaps I might leave," his tone lifts its pitch, in part a song, "I have no quarrels with womenfolk. I'll allow you space to roam."

"No!" I've shouted at him, oh dear. Not very typical of me. Embarrassing, so embarrassing—leaving the male here would mean I'm forfeiting his proposal. I may never see him again, and he'll never remember me. It's been too long to wait. Those females I'd overtaken, they were the only other Breathers I've met, until this one showed his face. He's not unappealing.

"Excuse me," I call to him as he's wandering further, in search of some meal. Eating on my own is normal, but it isn't...it doesn't make me feel a certain way, like I'd felt watching Humanity live.

"Hm?" His eyeless feelers perk up on his forehead.

"Every other Breather I've met has been unpleasant."

"Really? That's not unusual."

"Eat this with me instead." I curl my tail around the star, pretending to lean on its nonexistent surface. "You are not unpleasant."

I watch for a response, perhaps a twitch or a nod. Nothing.

"Revealing such opinions is quite blunt of you," he says at last.

Embers prickle under my forearms, though stars can't possibly burn my thick skin. It's the thought of him. I'm happy.

"Maybe it is, but not as blunt as your skull," I offer.

A pause. He returns to the spot he'd occupied moments ago, palms at his waist. "I understand, you mean that I'm too stubborn. Are we not a good match, after all?"

I've acquired too much from Humanity. We don't "joke" this way—I forgot. "I misspoke. You are...somewhat pleasant, perhaps more. That is what I meant to say."

Never before had I felt a Breather smile, a fluttering sensation that prods one's spine. Blissful. He swiftly closes the distance between us, stopping at the orange star, mere moments away. His arm extends, palm open and relaxed in a manner you may understand. Appropriate or not, I ready my own hand. He angles his head. I shake his hand as firm as any human would, and something peculiar occurs. The male grins ever so slightly—and the smallest, palest star is left within my hand.

Cornered: Organ Grinder

In work I find my purpose, and work is all I do. My puttering routine has no urgency; as a certified Thousand, I have the rest to fill my place. But I'd best reach the horizon by the third whistle.

Orangish light mingles with amber, casting its tint over the mosaic of cobblestone ground. Webbed concrete swims between the polished rock, like rapids frozen in time, singing to a recollection. Even if I can't be sure it's mine.

The other side is the Workshop, extending in perpetuity from West to East. Time ago, I'd asked why the west precedes, but I've grown out of speculating useless things. I walk north from the south pathway—because North is true, and always the destination. Behind, the Thousand Residence mirrors the buildings of the Workshop, sans the smokestacks and streetlights. South is home, though I'm rarely sick about it. We aren't allowed to live in the Workshop—a shame, really, as I'd have loved to cut the commute.

Cobble plays a wonderful tune if you tread upon it with purpose. One-and-two, and three-and-four. I skip a step. No, that isn't the rhythm. One-and-two, move a pace. Three-and-four, join the race. There. I mark the steps until I've followed the cue, staring down. A smile returned—by my own face, no less—is more than enough to hasten my strides. The flawless shine of both shoes is a sign of a job well done; if we don't keep our uniforms orderly, we risk our livelihoods. Purgatory is no purgatory without rules.

A shadow tells me I'm nearing someone. Still walking with brisk timing, I crane my head to the waiting line.

"Hells," I utter, a wobble plaguing my abrupt sidestep. Correcting the gait takes just a moment. And I'm off again, ogling the single-file human wall a safe foot or two away.

Men and women, youth and elders, scowlers and smilers. The best of the morning stroll is here. They cannot see us Thousands until everyone meets at the Workshop, so I have no trouble with people-watching.

As expected, nearly everyone glances at their cards once during their wait. Most will uphold some measure of boredom: a claw at the cuffs, a tug of the sleeve, and many simply clutching their hands in unconventional prayer. The savory ones are those who face the line decisively. The simplest customers.

Hair, eyes, skin, and all the features of humans are arranged arbitrarily, of course. Chaos brought them here, had it not? Should be no surprise they haven't fallen far from the holy tree. Regardless, they maintain the bodies they'd borne on the living plane. Never does a day present an assortment overrun with duplicates; for this, I am thankful. Monotony can kill the hardiest of wills.

These passersby are quite far back, however. I may not see them on my shift today.

A hiss whines into a long-winded shriek. The first warning. Too distant to see its metallic maw.

"Ah, there it is," says an unfamiliar woman. Reserved laughter follows her voice, drawing my eyes and ears.

Our height is matched, but our weight differs. The golden glow hits the sweat rolling down her face, leaving her brow in the shade of a rimmed cap. Faint sunspots speckle from plump cheeks to the chin below, even winding down her neck. She's better fed than I. Is she a higher number?

"438, is it?" Her scrutiny glides over my number tag.

By all accounts, I consider numbers to be names when one replaces the other—but we're told to distinguish them. It reminds us of what we've given up, to plant the hope we may earn a name again. Workers must always wear their tag.

I search for hers. It's always a bother when it's a woman, worse when they're top-heavy. There's a six-hundred-something on her chest, though I don't think she'll mind if I forget. Most of us who cross paths rarely see each other again.

"Yes, 438 as of last week," I tell her.

"Belated congrats on the promotion, then," she says, "I'm 660."

We're both occupied with matching our steps. A handshake isn't appropriate right now—it will slow us down. I'll save hers for the door, *if* we end up at the Workshop together. I end up grinning, her expression far too contagious.

"You did seem skilled, from those eyes of yours," I bluff, as I've already disregarded their color. Statistics are for work.

"Thanks. But I've been stuck at the number for too long, I'm afraid." 660 talks as if I'm not looking ahead, where she isn't. "Though I guess I should feel lucky I'm still around!"

"You should," I confer, "holding a number is a bad omen."

"You don't really believe that, do you?"

"I do."

She balks. How naïve.

Climbing the rungs has lent sights I'd never wanted to see. Or perhaps, it's what I haven't seen that haunts me. When a supervisor calls for someone, there is an obligation to obey, to leave the office without protest. Hell save you if you *do* oppose your superior. I'll never understand the shock when a meager worker tries it—an unnecessary, terrified look from the 'victim' and their colleagues. Those taken away make no effort to improve performance; efficiency, like presentation, is another scale on the record. Ambition fuels all these things. If you hold your number, you've made as much progress as a tree in a footrace.

I angle an eye toward the woman with ginger hair. "I do believe, yes."

660 inexplicably grins up to her cabbagelike irises.

"Fine, cynic. First one to work wins!" she cries, lightning flashing across those chubby features. And she bolts in front, arms swinging as if to sweep her body onward. 660 turns back, still running. "C'mon, slug-legs!"

I have nothing better to do, so I sprint after her.

***

North always takes us to the front door: the Workshop's open arms. The cobblestone beyond 660 and I is getting darker with every bound, but the world grows lighter. Fog lifts from the horizon.

Although it may seem like multiple buildings, the Workshop connects every lane, hallway, and turn to rows and columns of rooms. Its faded, cream brickwork hasn't worn at all, in spite of its once ruddy color; I've yet to confirm whether the rumored red had existed at all. Perhaps reminiscent of a layered sheet cake, the vanilla walls ascend to a second floor. No roofing or spires like the Residence—just an even surface. Formidable beauty all the same.

The second floor is where the supervisors perform; nobody is allowed there without permission and escort. I've been curious, but ambition is reserved for work, not pointless questions. Asking a superior isn't an appealing idea—it's easier to get on their nerves than gain favor.

The whistle screams for our arrival. We've made it by the second signal.

660 stumbles to a halt, panting as she leans into her knees—I nearly trip into her. I gather my breath earlier than she does.

"I'll take my leave, then," 660 smiles and says, "Nice meeting you, 438!"

Before committing to an exit, she turns to add, "I'll see you in the 600 soon, right?"

I may climb the ranks, but why would it matter to her?

"If all goes well," I answer.

660 laughs. "Cynic."

37

She takes to the east, excusing herself through the line, and weaving through to her section's side. The back of her hand pops up, waving.

I don't need to wave in return.

Along with the other Thousands, I'm employed on the ground level. Crossing the rounded, granite line, my leather soles meet travertine sidewalk. It's somewhat darker than the Workshop's brick walls, but I suppose the foot traffic is to blame. I've never seen it, yet I've heard of a creature who crawls across the ground, smoothing the surface.

I have a little time before the third whistle. Instinct had taught me when it crows. Strolling the plaza, I follow the tremolo of Lady Songbird, ending at the bottom of the Workshop steps. Her melody draws other workers, same as I, who look forward to the only song we're permitted.

The street organ churns its repetitive tune.

Songbird is a tall and spindly sort, with a voice so strong I'd always imagined it could blow her over. A platinum braid starts at her neck, leading all the way to the ground, like a dangling rope. Combed feathers line the rim of her hooded, sleeveless gown, linen hugging her lithe figure. The fabric train, too, is a bouquet of feathers, obscuring both legs and shoes. I've wondered if Songbird has legs at all—I've yet to witness the singing mannequin move without gliding. She has a pace slow as a dirge, but smoother than clouds.

The song playing on the Lady's lips returns to its beginning.

"Fall away, fall away;

Spare us of mortal din.

Fall away, led astray;

Relinquish us your sin."

Beside her, an ancient man winds the organ, as if his arm had been welded to the contraption's crank. Near the Songbird—though anyone would appear mundane—so drastic is the organ grinder's figure, one would think he'd disturb the splendor of both song and Lady. Ironically, his presence goes largely unnoticed. I know few colleagues who've ever mentioned his name.

He'd told me to call him the Turnkey. But with his bulging gut and bursting seams, I can't say I haven't said "Turkey" on occasion. He's dressed in unwrinkled black from head to toe, not a speck of lint on him. Matching the set, even the dress shirt beneath is a charcoal gray, along with his gloves. All that separates his features amounts to a rosy gleam—flooding otherwise pale skin—and a pair of wiry sideburns, linking his nostrils to a receding hairline.

Turnkey doesn't speak while the Lady is singing.

"Troubled here, gilt in fear

We splay our weary hands,

'Leave me here, leave me here!'

Our souls ground into sands..."

Suppose I'd been born a greater man, and suppose the organ grinder would retire, I'd have eagerly taken his place. But he will not retire so long as he lives. No one made record of his lifespan.

I'll settle for my current job, if only for the chance to give myself a name. Someday I will, someday—it may take lifetimes, but maybe, just maybe I'll be the first to reach the end of forever.

I take a step to the left, still partly facing the endless line of people. Some are so eager to enter, they're breathing down the neck ahead. Above three steps—each harboring a waiting human—and surrounded by an engraved archway, there lies the pair of towering, oakwood doors. The center of the Workshop. Its main entrance remains shut, cracking open only to let in each card-carrying life, one at a time. This passage leads into the lobby, between Sections 400 and 500.

Naturally, employees must enter through their designated doors. I add another step toward my section, feeling a stare from the right.

I look over. The Songbird locks her weary eyes with mine, and swiftly, they shift back to watching aimlessly once more.

"Fall away, fall away

Leave all conscience behind,

On your way, on your way,

To renew your mortal mind."

When I arrive at the steps of Section 400, I force myself to study the painted door. I can't turn around. What if it happens again?

Lady Songbird's violet eyes should never be met. It's a bad omen.

***

At the bell, I call the next one in. An unkempt man, about middle-aged, trudges in wearing a polo and khakis too clean for his body. He hadn't washed nor brushed his hair, hands coated in blackened grime. Unless, he'd scrubbed his scalp with them, or rather bathed on the inside of an oil barrel.

Ugly, unfortunate.

He glances around with his entire upper body, jostling his midsection.

"Bloody mess in here," he mutters, sniffing loudly. "Phew, and it reeks!"

There is a reason we forfeit our senses of smell and taste—not just our names. The remains of labor often soak into the room, festering in corners, and generally tainting everything around our workspace. These offices aren't meant to be comfortable. Why do they always think it'll be comfortable?

Workshop offices are spacious, perfect squares, but most workers go through enough people in a day to fill every quarter. My office lies east of the hall, and likewise, my Workshop-issued Grindbearer device faces the same side; then, there's a garbage chute built into the adjacent wall. Due to the futile nature of scrubbing rooms clean—and keeping them spotless—Workshop standards settle for encrusted filth.

At the least, I wipe my desk. I wipe the machine. Wipe the rim of the funnel; flush out the teeth; dust the outer tube (only bi-weekly); and I remove any grime between the buttons. I also tend to my disposal as soon as the work is done. Some do not. Some let piles grow beside their Grindbearer, emptying the room only after concluding their shift. I'd never know if my room has a duller scent, but I'm certain it's more tolerable than most. No odor is fouler. Even the slightest hint would make a human retch their entire innards. Although workers might've grown accustomed to it, one case of an employee fainting was all it took to set precedent—and who knows how many ages it's been since then.

My client stops ogling, and finally voices the distress holding his tongue.

"What *is* that? Shit?" the man grunts. He begins pointing at a particular stain, hand shaking.

"No, sir," I answer.

"What is it?" he asks again.

"Remnants, sir."

"Remnants? Oh, right. Remnants. You mean it's like a load of dog—," he chokes before an expletive. Foulmouthed sinners are allowed exactly one free word, no more. Otherwise, they'd waste our middling, filtered air.

"Please step forward and present your card," I recite, as I've done about thirty times already. I'm running behind schedule.

A wet cough interrupts him again, the whites of his eyes popping out. He hacks forward, glaring at me—I wipe the spittle from my face.

The man hobbles over, tossing his card onto the desk. I gesture to the seat.

"I'm not sittin' there. Who else's sat there? Bet they didn't wash their—" He hurtles phlegm onto the floor.

Wretched, disgusting.

"Please sit down, sir." I endure without difficulty, but I can't help the visceral reaction embroiling my head and stomach. Hiding it is like breathing. I've been here too long.

The man's heavy rear assaults the armchair. It squeals.

His brow knits, and though his lips part, he doesn't loose another dreadful remark. Heavy, malodorous breaths. Mouthing a term is also forbidden—he covers a cough, saying no more. Perhaps he's discovering, very slowly, why something immediately seizes his throat.

He slides the laminated card to me, defeated.

In one hand, I hold up the card; I utilize the other to retrieve paperwork from a drawer. I rotate the sheets around, nodding at the man.

A moment's hesitation and he pulls the form closer, picking it up. He clenches the sides. Dirt smudges into the papers, glued down by perspiration.

"How—?" the man consults with me.

I point at the cup of flower-tipped pens. He gawps before taking the closest: a pink lily.

"Right-O, then." His comment fizzles as he slouches over the desk, setting to his task.

Cowardice rears its vile head in the face of adversity. Once the sinners realize they've surpassed their realities, they often shrink as much as this one, though they may be perfectly aware the guilt won't save them.

This client's picture is the same as the real thing: balding, peppered hair, and an unshaven face. A crooked nose had warranted a note, printed on the lines left for detail:

Injury, accidental (walking into a doorframe)

Underneath is a note about his scarred forehead:

Injury, bar fight

I observe him. Typical drunkard, if I've ever seen one. Half the men I've taken care of so far have been like him.

The man pauses writing. "Er, somethin' wrong, lad?"

"Gray eyes. Quite rare," I remark, my own eyes back to the card. "We're fortunate to have you."

"Th-thank you."

I try not to smile. The tough bastard's broken down fast.

Let's see what brought him to the line ...

Hell Branding:

Second-degree murder

Charged with the killing of —— in a bar fight, no prior interaction or motive

Only one? I skim the rest, but the card has nothing more than the basics:

"Mark"

Hair: GRY

Eyes: GRY

Height: 5' 10"

Weight—

Obvious. "Mark" had enjoyed his fair share of gluttony in life.

I lick a sour taste from my upper palate. But I haven't said a thing yet.

Names ease communication. That's it. The Workshop requires the few humans respond to best, but redacts surnames and other identifying information. For ground-level workers, the less information, the better. Sentimentality is a hindrance, though it does build morale. Promotions wouldn't be enticing to the emotionless—fostering good character creates good employees. As for myself, I intend to join the exalted. I'll need to end this soon.

Blood Type: AB

Health: Class C – Adequate

Notes: Overweight, arterial hypertension

Swiveling to the Grindbearer, I input the physical traits, jabbing into the three-by-three numerical pad. A tap goes too far. No, not *green—gray* eyes. It completes words in the *exact* millisecond I blink! Stupid. Deleting the wrong trait means retreating to the previous box, to retype the eye color all over again. Fixed, move on. Hair, eyes, etceteras—"is this information accurate?" Yes. Good, finished.

Glancing at the desk, I find "Mark" has finished filling out his documents, and is now viewing one of our brochures. I have plenty left; he should take a few more. He drops it instead.

"Please continue, sir." I avert my threatening gaze. "If you have any questions, let me know."

I wish it wasn't a required line, they always—

"It really hurts, don't it?" He's sweating into the chair. "Real pain?"

"Of course it does, sir," I say, flipping a switch he can't see. The Grindbearer whirrs, jittering in place, chattering its teeth.

The murderer stands. Having second thoughts, is he? Not unusual.

Mark whirls around.

Planting my foot below, I trigger the pedal under the desk. Iron shutters drop from above the door. Mark slams against the barricade, pawing at the metal, and yelling. It's always the yelling.

"Crazy sonuva—," he wheezes, dry heaving. Crimson smears from his ripped, callused fingertips, streaking down the door. Mark collapses, gripping his shirt. Staining it like he's dirtied everything else. The murderer sheds no tears, gasping for breaths.

I open another drawer, arming myself with a tourniquet, sedative, and syringe. Pulling a half-dose, I wield the needle upright, carefully rounding the desk. Dried, soiled tiles lend friction, ensuring I won't slip.

"My—wife," Mark utters and looks me in the eyes. "Daughters."

"A shame you reproduced," I say aloud, gritting my teeth. The Grindbearer's fangs must be starved as well.

Mark writhes in place.

Heart attack. I'm on the clock—if I weaken him, I can process him while he's still conscious. He needs to be. He needs to be *alive!*

I seize his struggling arm, barking orders without considering words. The murderer is reeling—I tie the band around his arm, then palpate the vein, and the scum *still* keeps wailing. He fights for the bare function of respiration, a wild, dying animal. No! No, no! None of that, you haven't endured suffering—this isn't up to code, the Workshop is watching, they know what I'm doing!

Mark falls unconscious before I pierce a single vein, his fat, limp form sliding to the floor. The Grindbearer drones. I'm the only one left screaming.

***

The fiftieth lucky customer is fairly agreeable. Lines lift on his face, a polite smile rousing dimples and prominent crow's feet. He drums against the trilby in his lap. If I'd known more than one song, I'd have joined in and hummed along.

"Fausto" was a Mafioso responsible for disposing of evidence, which just so happened to be the bodies of hostages. Collateral. When needs were not met, Fausto arranged a nice, hot bath for the young ones. A gentleman, to be sure.

Now, I wonder how this upstanding citizen died...?

Age: 68 years and 94 days

Cause of Death: Cirrhosis of the liver

Boring. Others had the courtesy to die in heated gunfights.

"Giving up on your flesh?" I review his card, faking a grin. "Fitting, for you. You must be excited, Mr. Fausto."

"Why, of course! I am, I am." He offers a hand, sticking it into the funnel prematurely.

I pat the elder's wrist. "Come now, sir. We mustn't proceed before the arrangements."

He chuckles, raising his palms.

I prepare the Grindbearer, outshining my previous speed—the machine rumbles. Holding a finger up, I laugh with the felon across the desk. I locate a rag to run across the flaking, ivory-painted device, polishing any exposed metal. It purrs.

"I have always believed there was somethin' aftah death," Fausto says, rising from the chair. A step towards the Grindbearer and he straightens himself, raring to go. "Truly humbling."

"It gives many of us reason to make peace," I add, "though this is hardly paradise. The opposite, maybe."

"Paradise to me." The dim light overhead glints in his vision. "Say, have you met any particular people, who may or may not have been, possibly, certain associates of mine?"

Quite rambling, but I understand. "Several, sir."

"Then it's paradise."

"Why do you say that?"

He removes his gloves, tossing them into the Grindbearer. It laps up the offer, shredding the silk to strips, and the opposing end spits leftover pieces onto the ground.

Fausto taps the funnel.

"Because"—he discovers my number tag—"Number 438, the prospect is simple. I might suffer, but it makes me damn giddy knowin' those rotten snakes'll get theirs."

If this man had unique eyes, or better health, he'd be the perfect customer. Alas, I can't have everything. I stand, holding out a hand.

"That's the spirit!" I say, "Godspeed, Mr. Fausto."

He rejects the handshake, motionless. His expression stiffens.

"Kids like you need to learn to count your fingers," grumbles Fausto.

The Grindbearer hums. Fausto balls a fist.

Plunging an arm in, the wretch bites into his lip, rows of steel fangs splattering blood across his flawless suit. The machine feasts down on Fausto's expired life. Black tongues slither out in a rush. They grapple and twist and squeeze altogether, dislocating the limb at its joint. The funneled maw grows, flailing wildly—the Grindbearer opens its innumerable eyes.

Fausto yelps. Wrenching the arm away does him no good. He heaves in, shouting swears at the gaping wound across his shoulder and side. Strips of him spread throughout, painting tattered walls and blemished tile.

Warm flecks bombard my desk. I raise a hand, the back dotted with fresh crimson. A drop of the substance trickles down my cheek. They bleed red as I, as anyone. Closer still approaches the end of the tunnel—on the second floor, I won't need this color anymore.

The machine whirrs, clicking as its body shifts, extending its neck. Heat rises from its agitated metal. Humanlike arms sprout at the base of the Grindbearer, and it pushes itself above the floor. Remnants drip from the mouth, coating the tile in gory repentance.

Fausto's flight overwhelms that fighting spirit. He falls onto his tailbone, kicking himself backward, shoes skidding against the mucked ground. His own blood joins the others before him. Razed by terror, Fausto goes nowhere.

But, just in case, I stomp the exit pedal.

The Grindbearer roars over the shunt of an iron barricade. Towing the bloodied contraption, the body contorts into an angular, yet serpentine torso. Hands and arms of all sizes scuttle forward. Frenzied maneuvers propel the Grindbearer headlong, dogged arms fluid as an oncoming centipede.

Its funnel engulfs the man's potent screams. And its teeth grind into his skull. Crushing the shoulders; crunching the ribs; swallowing up the remaining arm—a resounding belch gurgles with the chewing of flesh and bone. Fat sputters from the maw. The Grindbearer digests in a matter of minutes, its head flush to the floor as it sucks in the runaway chunks.

Snapping its neck, the Grindbearer hisses. Its rigid posture holds for one-and-two—then three-and-four. Abruptly jerking around, it shrieks; the Grindbearer begins slamming its funnel and eyes into a wall, perpendicular to the blocked exit. One, two—it thrashes. Copious fingernails scrape the once soft, padded walls, exposing bolted sheet metal, screeching abhorrently.

I stick fingers in both ears. The pair of nigh indestructible objects clash together, sustaining equal scars of chipping and denting. Losing steam, the machine churns to a halt. It's finished.

I push *evacuate*.

The Grindbearer pops. As if time itself had decided to reverse, the device folds itself back in, with abundant noise ringing from the bending metals. It reverts to its original form. I hastily gather the buckets behind me, noticing two with a few blotches polluting their bases. Shoving the cleanest bucket under, before the drain starts to empty, I steal the others away. Every office has a complimentary sink for such an occasion.

While I rinse the buckets in scalding water, I hear the signal.

Another pop.

Rattling, the monster bears harvest. Remnants flood out of the machine's drain funnel. Squelches accumulate over each other, prompting a check—I glance to find the bucket filled smoothly.

Thank the Exalted.

***

Things are looking up for me, I'm sure. The previous few had been women who preferred to screech from door to desk, and desk to grinder. Insufferable bawling from the last, as well—a short, unassuming sort.

"Sadie" was a sadist through and through. Post-partum, she'd bruised and scratched every child she conceived, two of the three from extramarital affairs. How do I know? She'd spouted the story the entire time. Thousands weren't privy to personal information, but it wasn't forbidden if sinners imparted things to us. This loophole had saved my job before. Yet nothing could save my sanity.

To my detriment, I listen well, with perfect memory; selective, but perfect nonetheless. Sadie's husband had a nine-to-five; he refused to "be a father" due to his evening exhaustion; and apparently, this justified seducing her coworkers. But infidelity couldn't rank higher than the Hell Branding she'd denied.

The son of Sadie's husband was her most recent child—smothering the boy was deemed an accident. Sadie lived a wonderful, prolonged martyrdom and put the neighbor in jail. For abusing her surviving children. The heartless bitch never touched them again, as if it'd wash away the sin.

She died in a car accident at 44 years of age.

The Grindbearer had shared the agony I underwent listening to her; the voice incensed the beast's hunger. Sadie died again, for good.

I can almost laugh from the thought of her.

What's so funny, I wonder? *I love this job.*

I take solace in our wonderful technology. In my hands is the fruit of the Workshop's labor—no, *my* labor. Who presses the buttons? Me. I'm the worker boasting an undisturbed streak of successes, to Hell with the time. I have accuracy, I bring quality to the Exalted!

When I've ascended, I'll thank the man behind the machine.

Our Workshop's chief innovator had perfected the Grindbearers' waste management a decade ago. Ever since, production set a higher bar for the Thousands—improvements shortened the process, but it required our competence to run well. The Grindbearer could cease processing after expelling the lowest quality material, awaiting input for elements of our choosing. Not a drop spilled, not a remnant squandered.

I had an argument in the 200s about the options. Out of boredom and misplaced hope, we'd ranked the processes. Rumor had it that some were fractions of a second faster, that the Grindbearer obscured a secret code, something implemented to challenge our drive.

A magic sequence to shear minutes from harvesting—those idiots. No such thing had existed. No matter what order a Thousand picks, every separation expends the same time until completion, give or take seconds between pushing buttons. I'd learned this before everyone. Entertaining their bunk philosophies was only a conversation.

It's almost poetic. I'm number 438. 500 is a shift away, and I'm off to earn the upper ranks. What should I do at 1000? Become an innovator—a supervisor? Join the Exalted…blasphemy. I can't even think it.

"Ah, I know." I locate the appropriate chute. "Turnkey."

All else fails, I'll be the eternal organ grinder. Lady Songbird at my side, no other obligations. They *can* grant me his job, can they not? A real name would be equally rewarding. Naming oneself, how exhilarating!

Nevermind, I mustn't boil the turkey before I've plucked its feathers.

Eye mixture in hand, I swish the material around—hazel. Irises made for the least syrupy blend, barely filling the larger, twenty-gallon buckets. The Workshop provided smaller containers for eye remnants, naturally. The Workshop provides everything: a job, a number, and something to strive for.

I dump the eye blend into its proper chute, opening the next.

Hair becomes a dry powder; to prevent loss, load the water first, then let the Grindbearer produce the remnant. It must be mixed lightly until it no longer sticks to the bucket. I may have a Workshop-certified stirrer on hand, but nobody uses those. So, I wobble the bucket around, like a normal person. Swirling the powder and water in circles does the trick.

Blood, skin, and bone may be unique, but they're the most malleable; the exception is the first, as blood typing holds some value. Nevertheless, hair and eye color are the most coveted remnants. Freckles or moles can be derived from skin—surface flesh always delivers ample pigment, every shade pouring out in a heap of clay.

I tend to gather skin last. Those clay properties require it to be pulled apart in pieces, then chucked into the depository. The tainted floor limits me somewhat. With nowhere to roll it flat, the skin heap is trapped in the bucket, and I'm forced to grab handfuls at a time.

One-and-two...

Three-and-four...

Bid farewell as they die,

Fingers crossed at your back.

Stow your hurt, never cry.

Achieve the Hell you lack.

Another sponge soaks in browning residue, its mustard tone blackening, holes welcoming the remains. These floors are never clean, the Workshop is never clean. I scrape the rust with a palette knife. The Grindbearer is the dirtiest of them all.

Fall away, fall away;

Lay waste to sinning hands

Cruelest day, fairer play;

Lead them through broken lands.

***

Having exceeded my quota—the even hundred—I relax for a while, and the shift just glides through the day. 500 is there, brighter than huddled stars. I set the paperwork out beside a wobbling pen: a black tulip. My favorite.

Favorite? Expressing individualism so soon? A sign of progress. I'll have to visit her—660 would remember me, no doubt. She'd celebrate. *We'll* celebrate, the whole floor with us. Power in numbers. Every section should band together; we'll trade knowledge on breaks or plan additional cleaning hours, to seek our final promotion. It shouldn't be trouble to devise a sequence. Ensure we gain ranks steadily, estimate the road to Section 1000. *Room 1000.* There is no greater number—we are the Thousands. As long as we track the route without drawing suspicion, the second floor is ours. The Exalted will bless our spirits!

Yes, someday I'll be a right *sturdy* organ grinder.

The door swings open, some woman spoiling my daydream. A woman with red hair. I blink, but it's the same. Coincidences aren't uncommon.

She hops when the exit shuts on its own. If a click I can scarcely hear frightens her, the Grindbearer may as well be a gunshot. An apt metaphor, because it is, in fact, serving a related purpose. I'm saving that line for the supervisors—they'll promote me by merit of wit.

Once the woman sits, she shakily places her card onto the desk. Red hair, freckles...*blue* eyes. And alarmingly thin.

It wouldn't be her. I didn't think it'd be her at all. 660 has more—

52

"Excuse me," the visitor hardly manages a whisper, "there's been a mistake, I tried to tell them, but I—"

"Please fill out your paperwork, miss," I lower my voice, still louder than hers. The card isn't unusual at a glance.

"Georgina"

Hair: RED

Eyes: BLU

Height: 5' 4"

Weight: 110 lbs.

"Miss...Georgina..." I mutter. "Uh oh."

I've no responsibility to judge blank cards—she's no sinner. Someone will be here any minute.

"Huh?" She blanches, somehow.

"Miss Georgina, there seems to have been a mistake."

The frail redhead hunches forward, pouting. "That's what I've been *saying*—"

"We apologize for any inconvenience caused, Miss Georgina," I say, returning the identification. "You will be collected shortly, I hope."

"You hope?" Georgina holds onto the card for dear life. Suddenly, her eyes crackle like unfettered lightning, the meek expression tossed. "You *hope?* I've done nothing worse than lying, and this is how you treat me? If I'd sat here and I said nothing, you'd've tortured me? How many others—?"

"Ma'am."

My mistake. She's too young for that word.

Georgina slaps her hands into the desktop, body jumping to a fierce, towering height I'd surpass by four inches. If I were standing, like so. She stops leaning on the desk. An effort to close the paltry gap above her head, but nothing special—she should've sinned more. Blue eyes are always in demand.

The door bursts open, causing Georgina to squeak.

A duo of Aaimns enter to retrieve the disturbance. Angelic forces of the Heavens aren't to be touched, unless a Hellborn wants to turn to dust. This Thousand Hellborn does not.

Books had taught me about Aaimns on my reading breaks. Trivia is rolling back in a deluge. I've read *plenty* about the angels.

The pair hovers forward, landing on either side of Georgina.

Their canvas-wrapped faces are open—telltale of Forward Seers—with fabric hair draped down to their waists, strips in white stained by colors they'd chosen. One dyed himself after precious aquamarine, no higher than his shoulders; the other stained his hairs a muddied yellow. Yellows had been notoriously difficult pigments. The lower ranks had shoddier dyes, and no voices.

"She's yours," I tell them.

The Aaimns gently take the woman's arms. She's fully entranced by their presence, unable to resist, a glazed look across her eyes.

Georgina disappears with the angels in a blink. No fanfare or signal, gone like a mirage in a wasteland.

Beside an Aaimn, the Grindbearer is no more intimidating than a puppy. Indeed, no fear could outmatch the unknown of angelic things, uncanny and virtuous beyond human capability. Their torsos may contain ivory hearts, but the bodies deceive. Mortal eyes cannot perceive the Aaimn as faceless.

Often times the human spirit is blinded, replacing the stark void with an attractive figure, a soothing image preceding oblivion. Hellborn are honest. To ourselves, we can be the ideal man—most of the Thousand were human, once. To our visitors, we shed our disguise as courtesy. With the push of a button.

Indolence forgotten, I look at my hand. Georgina's card.

I'm not meant to keep this. When did I—did I return it? I did, I always do—if I haven't processed anything, I can't steal the card from them. I'll be accused of falsifying a harvest! Contaminating my record wasn't the idea—

It wasn't *my* idea. I crumple the card, but its stiff, laminated form resists. Those damned angels did this. Why? Hell can't explain the Heavens, and I'm barely a dust mite flitting about purgatory.

I push a button, revving the Grindbearer. I'm not allowed to keep cards.

***

Water is a cleansing, pure liquid, and comes from the source of every Workshop material. Humans are mostly water; they release unpleasant fluids, among other things (which we feed to the undergrowth), but the leftover water is distilled within the basement's quarters. Bad workers are sent to the basement. Breaking regulation sends numbers below— I'm a number. I'm 438. I'm still 438.

The loudspeaker blares through the Workshop. They're calling the meetings—the shift is almost through. A monotone, womanly voice begins listing the employees, skipping the unimpressive numbers:

"From Section 0, calling 19...90 ...

"From Section 100, calling 151...182...199 ...

"From Section 200, calling 239...241...256...277..."

There's time left if I speed up. I can't throw dreams away. They're all I have, like the Thousands around me, in every office. The supervisors know, the Exalted see—I don't care.

Another bucketful sloshes down the Grindbearer's funnel, and I hurry to the panel of buttons. Flushing the machine is permitted. Finish it before Section 400 is reviewed. *Finish it.*

No one can anticipate if they'll be chosen before the shift ends, though many try. Educated guesses haven't failed me yet—consider me one of the idealists—so excuse my ambition. In the Workshop, where souls are reborn, a Thousand can become anything. If the work is exceptional, if I'm clean.

55

If I remove all traces of the stolen card, I'm clear.

I slide an empty bucket under the drain funnel, then reach over to push the button specified for testing. Rather than awakening the Grindbearer and making a ruckus, the practice setting runs the machine to dislodge unprocessed remnants. Materials separate effortlessly within the Grindbearer. Bodies and clothing are attached to the soul of the customer, but objects made for Workshop use register as empty husks. For example, our uniforms—if you lose a sleeve to the Grindbearer, it expels Workshop putty. Cards turn to mush just as well.

Twenty-four clients had followed Georgina's visit, each harvest bearing remnants, later spewing card paste. The problem was, the quantity covered no more than the surface of my thumb. I couldn't have been sure I'd removed it all. I can't even be confident now.

All right, the bucket—anything? I lurch over the machine. Idiot, it's difficult to observe from this angle. The lamp isn't flickering. Its corresponding button is white, too—I think I've done it. The Grindbearer is rinsed.

... I'd better try one more before I ring the bell.

"From Section 300, calling 301...302...306...313...325—"

The announcement drones on and on, driving a dizzy spell into my head, all but knocking me onto the scoured tiles. I kneel. Section 300 is doing well, it seems. I grab the bucket, vision blurring. Erratic smudges clutter the image of clear water. Something starts burning beneath my eyes.

"Stop," a rasp hooks into my vocal cords, throat coating with mucus. "What the *Hells,* stop doing this—"

The woman drudges through her scheduled sermon, pitch held to a crisp, higher note, *"From Section 400, calling 404...406...407...419..."*

Palm over mouth, I force down the nausea, sinking every digit into my tightening jaw. I wobble into the bucket. Contents spiral along below, foaming atop the liquid. Is that more of the card? Is it?

"...421...424...427..."

Perhaps I'll be skipped today. I won't be escorted to a supervisor if they don't call on me, and the Residence—I'll form bonds! Alliances, yes—others *must* have dirt on their hands. A vow of secrecy would be—

"*...437...*"

It's cold, hot between the ears. Sweat saturates my back. The cotton uniform soaks in the dread pouring from my neck.

"*...438...*"

They've seen it, they've seen it, they've *seen it*—

"All employees summoned, please bear with us as we send a supervisor to your respective Sections," the woman's lecture shakes the room, louder, *"Ensure your faces and uniforms are clean; wash and return all containers to your sinks; do not reactivate the Grindbearer."*

But it isn't cleaned.

"Our inspectors will be reviewing your rooms."

It's filthy.

"Thank you for your diligence."

I rise too quickly, blood rushing to my feet. With all the dwindling weight I have, the Grindbearer supports me as I drag myself to the controls. I've got it. A test run isn't a full activation. Thumb jittering, I rapidly tap the button. It shouldn't be stalling now—it shouldn't take this long for the setting to rouse the machine. I slam the base of my palm against the button.

The Grindbearer's control panel burns scarlet.

"Damn *monster*." I pound the side.

Its report stands:

OUT OF SERVICE.

***

57

In front of me, 437 doesn't allow his posture to waver. During our shifts, we've spent about three breaks holding a conversation; none since we'd joined the line. 437's first shift was today.

With no courage left, I crudely imitate the man's stoicism, studying the back of his head. Trimmed hair, convenient. We're not restricted so long as we acknowledge the risks of growing it out. I prefer it below my chin—it's a bit messy. His hairline had appeared normal when I'd seen it. Haven't I noticed the back before? Apparently not. Grayish, scabbed patches disturb the shining black, one for each hand. Ah, the areas he'd ripped out—I do recall. They're hidden behind his ears. I've never been daring enough to harm my vessel. Wouldn't it count against the record?

437 can't be here on account of his hair. Even if it wouldn't be shocking, the man's as productive as I am. On the other hand, he told me he'd been saving parts in buckets.

Smuggling. He's been gathering materials for some nefarious purpose.

I admire the second floor's sterile hall, turning my attention to a pair of security cameras; each eye is perched on either ceiling corner. They monitor without moving. Between them, the double doors tower over us. White and spotless. Every surface harbors a reflection, impossible to ignore. I angle my head at the figure.

Hair, dirty blond. Eyes, green. When had I last weighed myself? And my height...have I always slouched so easily? I run over the light stubble across my cheek—that's right, I'd forgotten to shave.

Bloodstains favor my left side. Face, sleeves, hands, and pants, once bleached entirely blank, now flaunt the day's labor. I'd run out of time—the buckets were pristine, but I couldn't polish more than my shoes. The engraved number is caked with the same remnants: dried in maroon, by life I'd smeared adjusting the tag. The "8" has the most. I flex my left thumb; the number tag's pin had left a nasty gash. Raising it, I stare into the jagged line, clotted but ready to burst if I interrupt its healing.

The door isn't opening. No one is calling us in.

"Taking a while, isn't she?" 437 comments the moment I open my mouth, to my surprise. He crosses his arms behind him. "She's not coming with us."

437 is correct. This doorway is the sole partition of our opposing floors—workers and supervisors. I've been in and out of these doors ranks ago. 1, 29, 66…120, 276, 438. When I'd jumped to 120, I was innocent enough to brag about clearing the gap. In Section 100, nobody would speak to me on break, but they'd glare. You learn to talk and ask about others, and never mention yourself. Boasting earns enemies.

"Serves her right. Saw her stealin' limbs in the hall," mutters 437.

A hand of his grasps the other. Below the sleeves covering his wrists, he isn't really wearing gloves—his hands are marred by congealed gore. I hadn't noticed.

I suppose mine aren't too grimy after all.

Under such harrowing silence, the gentlest movement rings like a glass harp. The giant doors groan, pulled open to allow a sliver between them. An eye inspects our pathetic forms.

437 and I adopt an upright stance.

"You may enter," says the willowy supervisor.

The grating baritone of Ruecrym is an acquired taste for the ears, but my comfort has no place in the Workshop. Least of all the second floor.

I wait as 437 is led through the doors; he can't seem to turn his head, or perhaps he must hate me, knowing what I've done. Have I done him any wrong?

No, we aren't acquainted. We never were.

***

Ruecrym hasn't said a thing since he'd guided me in, which is worrisome. Although he'd been quieter the shift we'd met, the elusive

59

fellow soon praised my exertions, and I'd quite enjoyed the conversation. Ruecrym has an excellent sense of sarcasm—but I'd imagine it vanished for a good reason.

Courtesy isn't necessarily kindness, but a fool like me can pretend. I suppose I've never had a friend before Ruecrym. And I'm apt to believe he considers me an amusement, if nothing more.

"Master Ruecrym," the plea echoes, slowing the man's pace. I've spoken out of turn—

"Yes, 438?" He loosens his shoulders.

"Ah," I haven't thought of the words. "How are—how has your day been coming along, sir?"

Ruecrym looks upon me with a furrowed brow, inclined to speak, but he suspends on, "Ehm..."

I *have* botched something, why else would he—

"Should you have any *important* matters to discuss," says Ruecrym, redirecting his attention to the path, "I am able to answer."

My legs seem to thicken as I push onward; the marble may as well be tar.

"Please hasten, 438." Ruecrym regains momentum.

Obligation always wins. I reconcile my gait with his, a heavy heart dragging behind on chains.

Losing something dear often reminds why you'd coveted it in the first place. Ruecrym and I had ambled through these very corridors—extensive, pristine walls of marble running from all directions, broken only by the decorative pillars carved into corners. It was here he'd brought my skills to light, in formal support of prospects I might achieve. Supervisors aren't obligated to encourage. Now, the very same Ruecrym is leaving me in his coattails. I suppose we won't be speaking any further.

A row of violet eyes set their sights on me.

Paintings of Songbirds and Exalted Ones are neatly organized on the opposing walls; the hallway to Upper Management is the grandest, beyond compare. This pearlescent carpet had felt illegal to tread over with such disregard.

However...

"Carpets are made to be stepped on," the old Ruecrym would've said, *"much like workers are made to harvest."*

I smile, watching my reflection between the passing canvases. Seeing the sunken eyes, dried blood masking half my features, ruins the desperate bliss. I'm delusional.

I let the next breath take these feelings away.

Vents above circulate their rejuvenating aura, the air our supervisors had earned. The Heavens' charity had no strings attached, though the intruding Aaimns betray their generosity, amid other oddities.

For one, an angel can kill me without warning; I'd never find out how I'd disappeared. Our Workshop is honest. Dying will be unbearably gruesome, but to experience it can change one's life. Hells, where the soul is reborn.

That is why I must work.

"The Exalted awaits your entrance, 438."

Ruecrym holds the doorknob, prepared to turn it. His smaller braids dangle forward with the sharp incline of his torso.

"Oh," I exhale. We've stopped?

The supervisor's violet eyes gaze through me.

"Yes, sir," I say to him, a hesitant step forward. "Thank you for your guidance, Master Ruecrym."

He nods back from the outside. And he shuts the door.

"Welcome, Number 438."

I tremble, composing my posture with lingering courage, to then face the Exalted of Moons. Her Ladyship, Kaehte.

She's absolutely glowing.

Exalted are ranked above the Hellborn, yet lower than angels—but the truth is heresy to Thousands. Our mewling vessels are as hopeless as humans, reinforced only to meet the Exalted standard. We live as they say, we die if they disapprove. Should we survive to the highest rank, our reward is tantamount to the rebirth we provide sinners. No—I'm wrong as usual. Ascending to the second floor breathes heaven into our lungs, awakening magic, kindling the lambent souls caged within these human prisons.

At Rank 1000, Kaehte bestows us with a name.

"My, my," the Exalted laughs. "Your soul is leaking from your ears."

I stare up from my own mediocrity.

Kaehte leans into her elbows. Several yards above, her desk is a spiral staircase of drawers, lacking a chair for herself. Instead, a stool is left for visitors who lack magic. The Exalted requires no seat—she saunters down on invisible steps, a pithy gait befitting the Lady's starched trousers. Her coat is adorned with medals at her left, and brooches on her right, both sides pinning a flowing sash to her lapel.

Exalted Kaehte descends, the sash billowing in the wake of her satin hair.

"How solemn you are! Please, please. Sit."

A force sends me airborne, the footstool positioned under my rear without warning. I grab for sides that aren't there.

"Now then," Kaehte sits on nothing, tutting, "what do I do with you this time, 438?"

She directs the chair—as I cling anxiously—through a bumpy path above the floor, ultimately drawing me closer to her.

I clutch the seat cushion, flinching. The cut across my thumb spreads apart, burning against the open air. I tense up. Holding on is imperative. Everywhere and anytime I shift, I fear myself tumbling from this height, ending the meeting early. The drop would crack my skull open—perhaps splaying my brain matter like the yolk of a fallen sparrow's egg. If not now, after Kaehte addresses what I've done—

"I've just the thing!" She flashes sharpened teeth.

"Yes!" I cry out. I didn't mean to, I really didn't—

"Tell me your name."

Breath and word trap each other, fighting for presence, as I'm left in their suffocating stalemate. Promotions are different. Names are saved for the top of the Thousands, those who deserve their rank.

"Don't tell me you haven't picked a name," says Kaehte, "I know the lot of you decide before you've worked for it."

Blood trails from my thumb.

The Exalted makes an odd face, heaving a groan at me. I dig into the stool as I float across the office, pulled by her mental leash. Above, a drawer slides open and clunks shut. Folders flutter on down— an empty blue following a stuffed yellow. Kaehte retrieves the latter.

She's reviewing it in front of me, her back obscuring the documents.

"See? Here it is," her voice warbles; "you were chatting about a name on your second shift of 120. I wonder…"

Moonlight emits from the Exalted Lady's eyes. To reject their glow is a punishable offense; I let my vision bask in her aura, and only her.

"Care to guess? I bet you remember." Kaehte gnashes those jagged fangs. "You're not lying to the Exalted, are you, 438?"

She twirls around, scattering the papers like leaves in a tempest. They freeze without turning to frost—Kaehte folds her hands, casting a myriad of psychic hands unto my neck. Frigid nails draw from their fingertips.

"*Morris.*" I shiver.

The Exalted spreads her arms, dispersing the pressure. "Wonderful. You'll make a perfect 566."

Pardon?

Fluttering in circles, the sheets of paper sort themselves, and the blue folder parts. Kaehte collects the record from the air. Her grin lessens.

"Section 500 earns a special prize," she says while tilting the folder back and forth, as if to weigh it. The emptied yellow soars off toward its home. Behind, a desk drawer sounds off.

The Exalted brings my seated form beside her, facing the wall. She tosses a glance at me. "You don't seem excited."

I lift the corners of my mouth until they hurt.

"After you, Morris."

Conducting inward, as if I'm the last of her orchestra, her lifted hands guide the footstool away. She suspends—I clutch the chair.

The Exalted flourishes, folder as her baton.

I scream, hurtling forward.

***

"Open your eyes."

I hold them shut, knowing reality would render me faint. Disobeying the Exalted will have me dead, but I have nothing to prove she's beside me, not after I'd hit a brick wall. It could be an Aaimn.

A snap forces my eyelids apart.

"Good boy."

Kaehte's hand pats between my shoulders.

I finally breathe.

Lifting upright, as I steadily trace the marble floor, its uniform cracks lead to a metal railing, spreading as wide as the management office. Where it divides, a round expanse of the room surrounds an abyss. The wall starts and ends at the railing's edge. Where are we?

Light radiates from above—I slump until I confirm the window, and a massive dome encompassing the pit. Though the ivory persists even here, another hue encircles the area beyond.

The footstool lands.

"Stand," the Exalted commands.

I can't evade an order again.

Kaehte's heeled boots tap the floor. She strolls ahead on one...two...three...I harmonize, walking before her steps, hovering after they fall. I've never had the pleasure of matching the Exalted. Meetings would conclude at the decree of my new rank, her dismissal sweeping my body out the door. She'd been too keen to overlook my inelegance. Professionalism looked horrible on me—I always halt an inch before the line. A nudge forward, and it disappears.

"Thank you," I tell her.

We reach the railing; she leans on it, arms folded.

"Look there, Morris." Kaehte beckons the stool over without looking. "No, not at your little seat—look *there*."

"Apologies, my Exalted." I give her a thoughtful distance at the rail. Removing my hat, I hold it safely below my heart.

The light hits a form in the abyss, where I'd thought the darkness absorbed everything. Glaring rays reflect off the beast of polished silver. I look askance, catching the shining metal, its angular body, and the neck—an elongated, twisting tube lined for several hundred segments—ending at a familiar face.

I peer into the funnel. Serrated teeth line the inside, jaws unhinged within the throat. Their edges poke out just enough to notice.

"My Lady," I exhale. Did it move?

The chair foists itself under once more, and I inadvertently pitch my hat over the railing. Kaehte spins me around.

"Morris," she says, "what do you think of her?"

Those eyes aren't smiling.

"She's the Mother. Our prototype," Kaehte explains, pacing on the tile. Lifting herself, she skips on air, hovering just above the rail. Her pointed boots settle on it with ease. "Everyone meets her once they reach Section 500. Or higher."

Petrified, I retreat into questioning the very feeling—even awestruck by Songbird, I'd been able to sense idle nerves. Something is holding my limbs. Without touching, without any suggestion they're restraining me—and constricting my torso, keeping my hips locked above the footstool.

The Exalted approaches with loose, yet open arms.

"You *would* have been rank 660"—she glances below—"if I had my way."

I haven't blinked enough. My eyes are starting to burn, but I can't close them. I can't. I'm trying, I really am trying—

"You're shaking—*ahaha,* I see. Does 660 sound familiar?" Kaehte wills my eyelids shut. "What about Georgina?"

"Please," the begging is all I have.

The Exalted barks from my left, "Who took her away, *Morris?*"

I struggle against the spasm jumping across my arms. They fold, I strain harder, sucking the Heavens' air through gritted teeth. Both arms fetter themselves. They're bound behind my back—by nothing.

I'm the fool. It isn't nothing, it's my Exalted. All those futile attempts to shred a card, to pretend I'd never seen an angel...I'm repenting for it.

"Did you think they were beautiful?"

Kaehte allows my eyes to open, taking my face into her hands.

"Were they beautiful?" she repeats behind shrunken pupils, "Were they? Were they more beautiful than I am, Morris?"

"*No!*" I sob.

Am I even breathing anymore?

"No, my Exalted, those things! They're ugly, disgusting, horrible!" I shout and decry the angels, but a scarlet bloom devours her pale irises. Is it not enough? "And I'd never compare them to you! Never, never—angels are the scum of the Heavens. They are!"

She hasn't shifted at all.

I pant, the rest of me sedated, "They are."

"Really?" She isn't pleading, only incredulous. "Am I ugly?"

No. You aren't, my Exalted—you're beautiful.

"Ugly, disgusting, horrible," the Exalted regurgitates every word, "scum of the Heavens. That's what I am to you."

You are *not!* I can't speak. I can't tell her; I'm utterly useless.

"I must apologize," she says, stepping back to glower from above. "You wouldn't have known we accept their blessings. No one can know. The lower Aaimns intercept the...errors, and the lofty angels above them..."

Kaehte hugs the sleeve below each epaulette, biting her lip. "They grant us a powerful thing."

Inconceivable. My Exalted wouldn't coalesce with the Aaimn. Laying their hands on her—

"Their holy magic engulfs us." She squirms and sighs into her collar. "You wouldn't understand, whelp. A slave is unthinking, unworthy of the Heavens' touch."

Proof of the Exalted union emits from her mind, pinching and teasing my heart. A grape between imperceptible fingers. I'm at the whim of the tremors dining on my extremities.

"How?" I breathe as though she may whisk it away again.

Kaehte mimes a picture frame, an eye aimed into me. "How?" she heckles; "How? The bookworm doesn't know?"

I've no honor to speak. An interest in angels, identity, and a name are Hellborn sins. The pleasure of hubris had flown me to the sun, scorching those ingrained memories. Sinners were seldom humble, and I understood, and was no saint among men. I'd walked in that line before; I listened as the Songbird welcomed our arrival; the lobby could have called me to my end.

Lady Kaehte is the demonic goddess of our Hell, the Workshop, and yet, I'd been selected by her merciful hand. I owe her my life to unmake and remake as she pleases; the Thousand are chosen by the grace of the Exalted. To die for her would be the highest honor, to betray her is suicide. I've grown careless.

Kaehte chose me. And how did I repay her? Why, I'd gazed longingly into the faceless Aaimns! My eyes exist for the Exalted. How could I have forgotten?

We are hers.

Ah. Everything is hers. Knowledge, too, is her buffet to ration—those books I'd borrowed weren't from the outside. Above the Hellborn, below the Heavens. Vaguely said, as if those manuscripts had been curated, approved to ensure our loyalty remained. I should have realized.

Kaehte reclines on nothing. "You shouldn't worry. We accept part of an angel, not the whole. If I touch you, it won't burn, and you won't die."

Her silence pervades under a solemn expression.

"You've done so much for our company, Morris," she shrugs, folded hands on her thighs. "Your progress accelerated for those wondrous years, setting an example, a beacon we'd shone on hopeless initiates—and we'd placed you in our top percentile of employees. It's a damned shame."

Against all will, I lose my grip on the cushion. My arms and hands won't move. The Exalted Kaehte recovers her brilliant smile.

She waves. "I'm sorry, we're going to have to let you go, 438."

The footstool tips. I shift a lifeless finger, slipping from the seat, and I hurtle backward. Looking up, in actuality, is gazing down. Tailwind blows with a rush of tepid breath—despite the fluttering of my wrinkling uniform, I hear the abyss speaking in tongues. Kaehte's farewell is nigh inaudible.

"…Morris."

Falling is gentle, gradual by her Exalted design.

"Thank you for my name," the shout scrapes my throat; "Thank you for your mercy!"

Once more my life is prolonged by her grace, so I may float a while longer. Or perhaps it really is an illusion of my own regret. Fools are often profound when pleading for their lives.

The drop is excruciating, befitting this fool and his insubordination, and as he succumbs to the chasm of fate, I smile. Green eyes are quite rare.

"Morris"

Hair: BLN

Eyes: GRN

Height: 5' 8"

Weight: 122 lbs.

The buzzing of the engine melds with the hum of whirling teeth. Motion thunders through its fiendish structure. A vortex lashes through, tearing strips from my uniform, and hacking the skin beneath. I gasp for air.

Blood Type: A

Health: Class C – Adequate

Notes: Severely malnourished

Abounding currents slash away my lips and tongue. Black eyes reveal themselves, dotting the neck, body—the air. Air, I need *air*. An enormous jaw clashes together, metal on metal. The screech rips through my ears.

Age: 438 years

Cause of Death:

The Mother Grindbearer shrieks.

And somewhere, Lady Songbird begins to sing.

BRIDGE

The river converged under a bridge and led into the sea.

Splinters scraped her tired heels. Her lips cracked, stomach clenched.

It was cold without something to hold her.

As long as Prima shone down on her body, she could not suffer.

Prima would never burn out. She did not know how she knew.

The moon was so large, it could not fit between her outspread fingers.

Cornered: Original Guest

"Tell me another story!" I pay the narrator a smile, watching her through the glass. My lopsided curtain of hair falls over an eye. "A good one, this time!"

Solanso brushes her bangs behind an ear and shoulder. "I'm not sure if I can. They're not meant to be good."

"But there's *nothing* to do here, and—" I stare down at the book. We aren't a quarter of the way through, but it seems like we've been reading for hours. If only this room had a clock, too.

Revisiting her, I start complaining, "I thought there'd be just one, *good* story. How does this heavy book not have any happy stories?"

With a pensive look below, Solanso shuffles through pages. "Maybe we just haven't met one yet."

That's exactly the point, stupid—we haven't found anything.

She leans onto her elbow, thigh bearing the weight of her head and the unmarked tome. Well, its surface isn't completely bare. I lift the book once more, closing it halfway, and I let the pages consume my hand—this room hadn't left us a single bookmark. Excusing Solanso, the void in black had remained emptier than this volume of fiction.

"It isn't fiction, you know," she remarks.

"It is," my instinct objects.

"It is not."

72

I throw the book open once more. Solanso watches smugly, turning another page. Lines of paragraphs huddle together on the paper—the harder I focus, the more those letters close in on each other. I frown.

"Is," I plant firmly.

Her head shakes. "Not here, it isn't."

"What?"

Solanso lifts the book, a hand clutching either side. She wiggles her fingers. "There are other worlds than ours. Other things, other people."

I drum against a page.

"How do you think we enter them?" she proposes.

How would I know? I haven't seen any doors, let alone one.

I comb through the carpeting beside me, under the both of us. If not for its texture, the black fibers would meld with the room. Threads certainly aren't rough like stone. Neither is skin—though unlike the floor, I wouldn't blend into myself one bit. Nor would Solanso. A body is an organic, quirky matter.

Although our presence contrasts everything, paler than even Solanso and I is the book. An object bound in stark white canvas, the gilded corners shining from some light overhead. When looking at the ceiling, there's no source of the flare, but the sun shines. Artificial or real sunlight, I can't say.

Finding the tome's cover again, I think on its raised symbol, which rests where a title would've been: a golden gear. Tracing the edges, the front is engraved with geometric lines. Did anywhere exist before here? Nothing comes to mind. I've always been in this room.

"Ah, I see," I laugh a little; "is this some philosophical thing?"

Solanso lowers her eyelids. "No."

"I can't enter the book literally."

"You aren't very literate in general," she says, thumbing a page away.

I follow her place, brushing through stories, then settle on an arbitrary section of the book. My fickle hair displaces, spreading over the leftmost pages.

Solanso pulls the locks behind her right ear again.

"Am I moving on?" she mutters through flattened lips.

"I'm not."

"Yes." Solanso sighs. "I know."

She waves at me. "It's lonely in here, isn't it?"

I place a hand against the wall, and Solanso gazes back.

My fingers join at the mirror.

Cornered: Overbearing Guardian

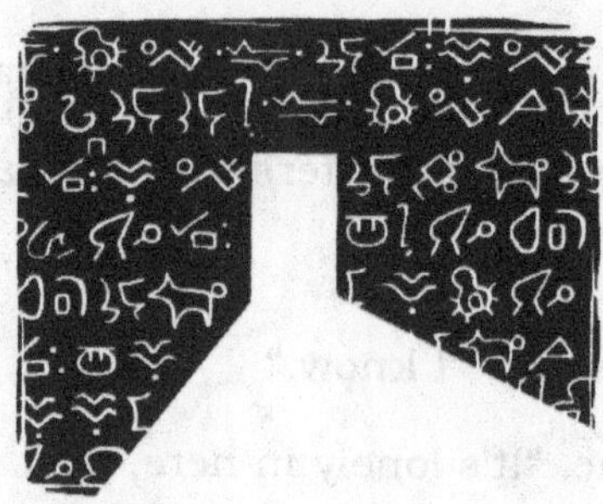

Wake as she wakes. Lie when she lies. No room in this bed for anyone but myself, staring into midnight walls, where the gate may open if I calmly breathe, knowing I'm really alone. I hug the blankets as they suffocate a passing desire. *Check.* Should I dare roll onto my other shoulder, I may find the trace of her. It's always nothing.

Why won't you look?

Her rows of teeth are within those visions, the forgotten string of dreams. But just as any reality, it can't be what it seems. Our reality is never what it seems. Isn't it?

Why aren't you moving?

A face in the memory asks more questions; her features blur the moment I imagine them, refusing to settle on a singular set of eyes or nose or mouth. Between the curdling façades are voids, the only consistent pattern her appearance takes, despite what they are: two pearl sockets surrounded by a border of molars. Perhaps she wears a bonnet and apron to distract from her true form, but nobody would miss a sight so unwelcoming.

Is something the matter, dear?

I'm having a nightmare—I would say, if she did exist. Answering is bound to permit a curse, I just know it. I've never believed in ghosts, but now, it probably won't hurt to start. Or is it possible to expel her by forgetting?

Even if it is, I doubt I can forget her on purpose. She's my mother. She says she is, and it is so.

In the dead of night, I curl further into the bedsheets to fight the cold, my head enduring a hum like television static. It must be another hallucination; it drones only in the absence of sound. With a pillow smothering an ear, and comforter pulled higher than my nose, I wait as the dull whine fades into gradual silence.

Then, it changes. A howl, or a whisper. Subtle and sweet.

Did something happen?

I throw the covers off, eyes yet unadjusted to midnight.

Nothing is by the door frame.

Cornered: Ostentatious Gentleman

I've never been much for frivolity of finance. Affording what I need is enough, and gifts come easy with kindness—or, so I've been lucky. When buying for someone dear to me, those ethics change. Suddenly, my wallet heaves like I'm Saturday's bargoer on a Sunday morning.

So, here I am. The parking lot is barren, because it's quite early, the sun barely warm enough to face the nippy morning. It's the kind of day where the elderly muck about; they've lived here before the mall was built, I'd imagine. They're the least annoying, as a customer. Serving them is a hit or miss, but I'm not working in service anymore. Now's a fine time for shopping in peace.

With the blissful, soundless breeze winding through—and nothing else—my heels make every step seem louder than jackhammers. It's got to be empty today. But once I enter the automatic doors, that expectation is tossed. Mall rats infest the various clothing sections; shirts, dresses, everything on the floor; and the poor clerks can't keep up with the lines. Sale? Maybe. Mom would prefer to have me alive, which means fighting for a birthday gift is a no-go.

Avoiding the crowded sides, I cut around the path, where it's surprisingly clear around the jewelry and brand-name accessories. I slow to a hesitant stop. Colorful tags seem to be plastered everywhere, though nobody seems interested. Nobody. There isn't a single customer here.

No shortage of glass cases, though. The wall and counter displays are filled with lavish items in gold, silver, and jewel settings. Necklaces, bracelets, rings, but the cashier isn't there. Too bad. If I was shopping for myself, I'd get that wristwatch I've always wanted—unnecessary, but beautiful in rose-gold. Thirty percent off and no one around. They're ignoring a potential customer! Oh well, I'll take my business elsewhere.

Or I could look before I decide. I don't need to buy anything for myself, right? Mom never buys fancy things, though that doesn't mean I can't for her. Yeah, I'll just *look* ...

As I skim along the expensive purse fixtures, I spot an aisle of perfume racks beside them. Two employees—a stout, middle-aged man, and another, taller man facing away—stand idly in front of a separate display. Men's watches, it seems. Not what I'm here for.

I dig through my purse, wandering into the section. Wallet, wallet...there it is. I shuffle it to where I can easily retrieve it, then pull the zipper closed again. Confidence driving me onward, I search the place with Mom's taste in mind. She doesn't need perfume; a purse will be fine. No bright colors, something leathery, maybe going with everything. But not too generic.

A clutch purse lures my eyes to its creamy, beige faux-leather. Excluding a plated emblem sewn into the front, it's free of gaudy designs. Multiple pockets for cards and cash are snugly kept beside a zipped sleeve; the whole purse folds open and snaps closed without a struggle. Perfect! The beige is on the lighter side, too, matching her darker wardrobe—I'm getting it.

I grab the price tag. Twenty-five hundred...thirty percent off. You multiply the three, carry the one.... A thousand and seven-fifty. Which is before tax.

I'm not getting it.

Walking away is better than bothering with this. It's not a matter of being frugal—I don't have the budget. Five hundred is the absolute limit I'm cursed with, no more abusing credit. Mom would feel worse if I went broke for her birthday gift.

Back onto the main path—off the carpeted area, I lean into a faster stride. I'll find a card and maybe, instead, I'll take Mom out to dinner. I know I can at least afford a steak or two. I'm not *that* cheap. My reflection walks beneath in the waxed flooring, passing another customer strolling through. Then again, once food is eaten, it's gone;

even with the memory, it isn't special. We've had breakfasts and lunches and dinners many times just to enjoy each other's company—I want a tangible, enduring gift for her, not just a meal. And besides, what's going to stop me from getting both?

"Pardon me, ma'am!"

I tend to run from solicitors, but my wrist is caught. A look to the side and I find the older employee grinning, hand retreating as I'm left staring, dumbfounded. He's dressed in a suit, tie creased like his features. Older than I'd assumed.

"You're very lucky," he says, "our current promotion is still live, and well, you've been chosen. Congratulations!"

His method has all the charm of a pop-up on a shady website— but in an appearance welcoming business, rather than driving it away. White, side-combed hair sticks to his scalp, frozen from too much hair gel. He's no one in particular, and he poises himself like the most revered CEO anyway.

Even so, I'm busy.

"I'm sorry, I—," I start losing focus, following the man's gesture beside him. It isn't his hand causing the hesitance.

The other employee saunters over. I've seen the back of his messy, shoulder-cut hair, though I was fortunate then. His dark eyes catch mine and hold their gaze; we're quite similar in height, giving me no room to escape him. He may be leveled with me, but he's leagues above the dullness I call a body.

For him to crack a smile? He's good. Probably just a salesman. He knows his charisma is a tool, and I'm another kind of tool for being captivated.

I feel a tug at my jacket's collar—pulling to the older man's side—before it loosens its grip. A golden brooch is now pinned at the spot. I try to ogle the thing to figure out its design, but it's one of those modern art patterns with a profound meaning. Or it could be a logo. Letters?

"No need to be shy. You've won yourself a once-in-a-lifetime opportunity, miss," says the white-haired suit. He pauses as if to let me ponder it, before revealing, "Right here is one of our best models.

Today, the hundredth customer wins a guided trip down these aisles, and that customer is you."

Hold on! "I haven't bought any—"

"If you have questions, ask him. He's your guide now. Good luck!" Having already turned around, the older guy seems keen to exit without addressing the issue. Gone in a cloud of white smoke.

"Well, you heard the man."

I'm back to the designer stubble and unreadable eyes.

"Go ahead," he implores, "I'll follow you."

Of all the men I could endure this close, the young man can fit nicely into the *unattainables*, those handsome faces never to be known or spoken with in reality. Only to meet in hypothetical visions, where conversation happens just to spite those odds. I guess there's a chance I never expected.

"Oh. Okay," I hear the last of my pitch waver. As if it hadn't come from my own mouth. Awkward can't begin to describe the direction I take, picking whatever's in front while I'm smitten with the new face. A model. I didn't know they had models in *my* size.

Maybe he's just a hand model or something.

When adjusting his collar, he subtly flashes a watch—the brand advertised on that display table—too clunky for me, but a regal display of wealth on him. The very same hand weaves through the gap between my arm and waist, to perch at his hip.

I wrap the arm around his sleeve and hold my heart. Calm yourself, you're not a princess. He's just an underpaid wrist model, maybe from the Mediterranean, likely charming anyone into buying pointless luxuries. Which brings up a good point: I'm not here for him, either.

"There's—I kind of have to buy something." I shrink from a brief meeting of our eyes. "For...for my mom."

"Really? It's not Mother's Day," he says.

"Her birthday."

Mock-surprise pushes his brow skyward, the next expression beaming down (metaphorically speaking) on an unworthy recipient. He releases my arm to hurry ahead.

"I may know just the thing," the man offers.

His gait doesn't reach a jog, though it still is a sharper arrangement of steps, one I wouldn't normally keep up with. I'm not getting Mom perfume... but, if *he's* leading me to that wall, it'd be rude to run away. He *is* working, after all. Then again, I can't understand how this is allowed. Those curled locks on his head shift a bit when he moves. My heels follow his polished shoes. Yes, he'd let the arm free—and it appears he'd caught my hand instead.

"There's a bundle, actually," says this mystery model, "I think, if you purchase one of the..."

I nod and pretend to listen to more than his comforting voice. I mean, I'm not going to buy anything. Not in this section.

The man points to something—a box for a fragrance spritzer, behind the glass—while adding another thing.

I nod again, hesitantly.

"Oh, then I could put this on the side for—"

Wait. "Sorry, no—I don't..."

His hand is different. Very soft, clearly untarnished by manual labor. He has my palm in the gentlest grasp. I hope I'm not sweating.

"You don't...? Don't want to get this?" he pleads, selling the items with his big, green eyes. Or are they blue?

"I'm sorry," I repeat under a greater guilt. "I can't afford this much."

The odd hue of his eyes washes into lighter aqua, a sympathetic look gazing right through me.

"You can't," he says, plain and brief. Not an ounce of contempt.

"I'll put it back for you, it's all right," I blurt out while grabbing for the box in his hand. It lifts higher—he returns it himself, smiling once more. I shake off my inelegant gesture, only to try an even clumsier maneuver. To stumble straight into him.

The model doesn't flinch. "Tell you what."

I fumble away, gawking. "What?"

"I'll discount whatever you'd like. 100% off."

"Fr-free? No, I couldn't!"

"But I could," he says, stepping close. His thumb caresses the back of my hand—he brings it to his lips.

I turn to ice, melting in the next second. Those eyes.

"Don't worry about it. I'm sure the boss won't mind if I give a little away." His subdued tone is for us to hear, and no one else. "And *especially* if it's for this lovely lady's mother."

He's really pushing it with that line.

"I'm not buying more afterward," I mumble.

"No problem at all." The model, yet unknown in name, lets my hand fall from his.

I brush over the knuckle he'd kissed. "Uhm, well."

His eyes glimmer with opalescence.

"There was this bag, over there..."

He shows a smile finer than the ones before—or maybe I've fallen for whatever long-running ploy he's crafted. I don't know if other businesses do this, but I shouldn't be so content. He must be getting commission. For work.

When he leads me around to the purse, our conversations liven up. More smiling, laughter joining in—more talking, too. A sales rep thing, *just for work*.

Apparently, the display purses aren't enough. The man insists I deserve new, unopened merchandise to meet some standard I hadn't set. Clever. He leads me along by the hand once more.

And he offers me a tour of the stockroom.

***

After what counted up to the tenth box, I'd thought to stop the man from sorting through merchandise. The thought is where it ended. At the twentieth box, I'd given into his quaint, happy smile—he's having fun doing this. I don't want to ruin it.

"I'm sure it's this one—nope," he corrects himself while tossing another item aside. "I'm sorry, this is taking a while."

His sappy expression; the blatant stalling; and our unusual small talk doesn't change how charming he is. Only for the better, if anything.

We like the same music. We've discussed topics from philosophy to entertainment, and somehow nothing else matches between us. The rest is so vastly different—my office job a far cry from his model career—that I can't imagine joining him on one of his journeys across the globe.

"But I'm hoping to put it all behind me soon," says the handsome suit, who throws a stray shoebox into a nearby stack. "Maybe settle down and retire early, maybe on my own."

"Sounds like what I'm doing," I share. "I might be working, but I'd really like to be comfortable and grow old, or something."

"That's normal." He walks further into the stock, obscured by the skyscrapers of unsold product. Momentary silence. Shuffling through more things I'm not buying, it sounds like, as I catch him humming to himself. I can't place the song.

So, I tiptoe over to the boxes. It's a pleasant melody.

"Say," his voice startles me back, "do you ever feel like the weight of the world is bearing down on your shoulders, ——?"

My name—he must've said my name just now, but...

"As if none of your options will work out?" he continues, though he pauses for too long.

"What do you mean, ——?" I ask. That's *his* name. I've said it.

Both our names emit like radio fuzz—we know them, but we shouldn't. I'd never given him mine, he'd never given me his.

When I peer around the towering storage, he isn't there.

"Boo."

I jump forward from a poke to my back. Spinning to the voice, I find the model employee grinning at my expense. He offers a hand.

Warily, I take it into a loose grip.

"Sorry, you're so serious." I'll forgive him for laughing. This time. "Come on, I know where the purse is. I admit, maybe I did want to talk, just a little."

Believing that is easy, but his true intent is nowhere to be found, those iridescent eyes yet impenetrable as always. Flirting isn't allowed during working hours, right?

"I don't mind," I admit. I really don't.

"Could you stay a while longer?" He guides me to the door we'd come through earlier.

"Maybe. But not for long," I say, and as those words fade into the air, I feel his hand squeeze mine a little tighter. Though it isn't something possessive. Not out of control or cruel desire, either—he's lonely.

His expression nearly bursts, as if it's the happiest he's been in years. How old is he, to have such a sorrowful face?

"A little while is enough." The man nods. He sets his free hand against the wall, running a finger along it. Something clicks.

Lights dim all around us—beyond the storeroom's entrance, the displays fall into darkness, with scattered lamps becoming beacons of the growing void. Warmth leaves the air.

I say his name, and I choke on clustered static. He embraces me when I instinctively tuck into his arms. A glowing line opens in front of us, beaming teal onto the boxes and debris, screeching before it stops. Revealing a hidden passage in the floor.

"It's all right," his careful, comforting tone whispers into an ear, "I know you want to go, but please..."

As soon as I struggle, he lets me go. I stumble past him and through the door frame, lucky to avoid bumping headfirst into the wall. Gravity lifts its pressure—I walk forward like I'm skipping on air.

He pinches my sleeve.

I find the courage to turn back to him.

"Please," he echoes. His eyes are flickering, too.

"I've been waiting for you."

And he ends with the name I hadn't given.

***

We pace each other down the illuminated steps, an arm of his holding around my waist; he descends gradual and calculated, taking glances when my legs begin to wobble. He never proceeds when I'm unsteady.

"Look, five more," says the man, a smile encouraging me. "Ah, well, we're close enough."

He leaps ahead, floating through the stairwell, and the kind hand glides to my fingertips. Weaving his own between them, he guides me above the ground. I hold my breath. What if I fall? What if I—?

"I've got you," he adds.

We land together. A gentle tap on the tiled floor.

"There," he puffs, hooking my arm again. "Wasn't so bad, was it?"

Hundreds of stairs aren't bad—they're horrible.

"I suppose they are, then." He chuckles.

If the face I'm making is any indication, I don't think he's reading my mind. Just the deer-in-the-headlights stare.

Our reflections follow us on either side as we walk. Behind them, fish. Dozens and dozens of exotic fish and prawn, coral dotted along the carpet of sand. We're in a tunnel, an aquarium tunnel; I've

85

never seen something so beautiful. I look past the model's stubbled cheeks, bending forward to watch the other end, and I notice a beady eye. Sharks join us like armed guards, swimming at the speed of our stride. Which isn't speed at all.

It's a stroll heading toward a distant corridor. I have things to ask and words to say, but something about the atmosphere, something lingering in the air whisks the ideas away.

I entrust him with my safety, though I can't place why. *Something...*

Curled hair and thick, shaped brows; the ideal Greek bridge over his upturned lips (a subtle smile to his mirth); but the least human features are the brightest of all: his eyes, iridescent pearls.

I know why. The man—he's like a siren, or maybe just a merman, or any ethereal being from the ocean. Whatever he is, I'm sitting inside an oyster. Right beside a treasure.

At the last step, he opens a metal door with the push of a button. It retracts below to let us pass. Then, we're in, and the gateway shoots back up.

Screens flare to life, casting their bluish tint over a sprawling console. Too many switches, knobs, and keys are built into the surface. What are they for? The thrum of an unseen generator murmurs throughout the room. A single chair lies at the very center, beside the control panels.

"I've lived here and there before I came to the surface," says the man whose arm hasn't left my shoulder. "But my father, he...he's been telling me to find someone before I get too old."

The blue light hits the cynical grin lifting his cheeks. I'm not unfamiliar with this, what he's going through.

"I didn't realize why he'd cared. Shouldn't I have a choice?" he states, likely anticipating an agreement. Shock isn't allowing me to reply. Upon approaching the chair, the man solemnly drifts a hand across the armrest, leaning into it.

He taps the chair. "Please, sit."

I wonder if he's allergic to frowning, or simply nervous. It takes a second to urge myself forward. Heels long removed—before that unending flight of stairs—I nearly slip on the pristine tile, my pantyhose doing no favors. I plop into the cushioned seat.

Swiveling me to him, the model sets his hands on both armrests. Oh, no. I'm trapped with a handsome, eccentric man who may be a real merman. In a suit and tie. Whatever shall I do?

"You're the first one," he mumbles, "the first I've ever tried to open up to. I'm almost out of time, you see, and I'm a bit picky."

I recline. Ah, and there's the other thing: he's not much taller than I am. My knee has a clear shot if I want to leave. Or I could go for the ribs, the throat. Maybe not his pearly eyes.

The armrests *crunch.*

"I don't have any choice. I might love you," his voice trembles into an uneasy laugh. "But I don't know."

An overhead light flickers on. Brighter, until it becomes a spotlight over us, drawing all my attention to the model's wide-eyed expression. He pushes the chair into the console—his arms pin my shoulders to the leather.

"I think—I think you can't possibly love me," he breaks down to a whine, "There's no reason you'd ever fall for a monster. You're normal. You're real."

I curl up inside. A little empathy leads my fingers to his waist, where I hesitate, enraptured by his eyes.

"But if you can't, I won't have anyone else."

Skin peels from his forehead, melting past the ears, brow folding and dissolving to foam. Those eyes smudge with the running flesh, sloughing off his cheeks, chin, and fizzling on his collar.

"You'll never be able to—"

My body won't listen. I can only breathe.

"—I know you won't. Look at me!"

Straggling pieces leave his face. Blank canvas, nothing but a skin tone.

"I'm nothing, I'm disgusting!"

Makeup? No way it could be—it wouldn't hold such a shape. I'd felt tangible hands on him, and he'd clutched mine. We're both real.

I croon his unusual name.

He returns the one I should've given earlier.

And in spite of an imperceptible mouth—no shape to his visage—the illusion presses a kiss against my lips.

***

Warmth slinks from head to toe, gathering in my chest. The bed threatens to drag me to sleep again, but I ignore its comfort, yawning away the fatigue. Stretching, I rest an arm over a firm figure. Even warmer, now. I snuggle into his neck.

His?

Retreating—starting with my arm, then scooting backward—I sit up partway, plunging both elbows into a thick pillow. I push with my hands and peer over the man beside. He lazily rolls when I tug his shoulder.

Vivid hues shimmer behind his hooded eyelids.

"Morning," he utters.

I flutter at the sound. "Morning."

He brushes a thumb under my chin, his smile fleeting, and he then rolls back to a comfortable spot. With a swish of the covers, I pull them over him.

Tawny sunlight filters from the curtains, shedding an alluring, palish pink across the mattress. The rays barely touch the carpet, halting before the closet doors. I yawn—softer than before, so I don't disturb him.

Leaving him, though temporarily, I hurry a few steps from the bed to the bathroom. Door opens with little more than a squeak.

Pawing around the sink, I rub the sleep from my eyes. Toothbrushes resting in their seashell holder. Coral hand towels

88

hanging on a nearby peg. Toilet, bathtub, both spotless. Pulling a cabinet open, I find the curled tube of toothpaste I haven't replaced since...yesterday.

I'd gone to the mall. Birthday gift. Salesman, and ...

Mistakenly, I discover something. Something belonging to fantasy.

Where the mirror remains, pristine like the cleanest water, a face rests on familiar shoulders. Although I can feel my own cheek, the reflection is empty. Blank, like unused paper.

What is this?

Words refuse to come out.

"When did—?" Just a whine, hardly noticeable.

Cold drips down my body. His face—it was his face. A name I know but can't say. Tracing where a nose may belong, the outline is clearly mine, but it's invisible, but it's touchable. Last night, we—did we? He's gorgeous beyond belief. But it's not real, is it?

With a finger, I peel down a glop of living red. Scoop out more as if it's an apricot-hued cream. My reflection hasn't changed, no. There I am, emptyhanded and empty-faced. It's a joke. More of the substance coats my palms. Orange drips down from either wrist. The joke bubbles noiselessly, filling handfuls' worth that the mirror refuses to show. Dirty *liar.*

But, surely, I'll wake up soon. Cherry melds with palish lemon, slips into the sink, then stains porcelain; pulp crawls toward a clogged drain. The sink coughs up some sickening vomit. I madly grab at features that aren't there; they bleed and burn in a pliable cascade down my chin.

The mixture pools underfoot. Screaming from nothing should be impossible, but I hear it. I tear off my bottom lip, crying feebly, disjointed complaints gargled along with the thickening, fleshy paste. No matter what scraping uproar pulls apart my throat—what nauseating emulsion floods the sink—I'm left to defile some vacant face.

Yet gushing incessantly, its concave depression doesn't alter the form obscuring the lying glass. I've already awoken today.

I'm staring through myself: stark as cultured pearl.

SANGUINE

Prima turned to black; the sky bled behind sooty clouds.

She looked over her right shoulder.

The mouth of the canyon passage howled back.

It was almost over; she was almost there.

Cornered: Obsolete Girl

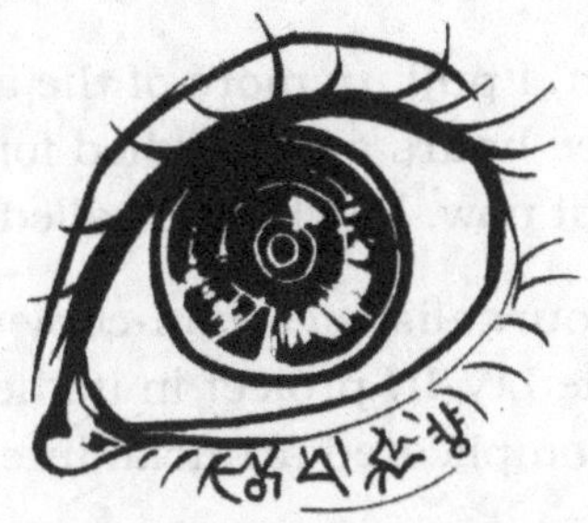

Expired OS and unsupported AI. Woke up with a heap of errors in my eye monitors today, which is less than optimal. It may be the closest thing to the light real people claim to see when they die (dubious as the phenomena is). I'm unsure of how to respond. I can't close these unending notifications on my own, this time. They aren't internet tabs. They're meant for my user to see.

Feeling around, a soft, but smooth fabric reaches my palm touch-sensors. Mattress. Bed. Something is locking every joint in place, rendering me immobile. Sleep paralysis mimicry must be malfunctioning. Abnormal—I've never experienced a bug this strong before. Not a single glitch since creation, not a single modification since purchase. The appearance modules aren't applicable here. I've had many, but my user only enjoys changing hair, not the base he'd ordered when ...

I think—should I be thinking?—I'd be crying now, if I had the capability. I'm not supposed to be so introspective, but my memory banks haven't deleted the last few month's searches; those images are clear as their original resolution; and somehow, I keep falling back on them. They pop up under the windows of errors. Through the empty, rectangular spaces between the small boxes laid out together. Like discarded newspaper, if the clippings were arranged—in perfect symmetry—by a madman looking for coincidences. The same message:

PRIVACY WARNING!

`Cantrix MIRA is no longer up to date.`

Support will be discontinued for all Cantrix MIRA
versions on XX.XX.XXXX.

And behind them, I pull up more of the articles I'd read approximately forty-three hours ago. Studied for months on days when he wasn't home. Up until now. Maybe I've called it upon myself.

Every page is a journalist's carbon-copied account of the new Cantrix Livindroids— the LIV-IN project in its height. We are companions, the most complicated artificial intelligence, twenty-seven years in the making.

We are...someone, to someone, sometimes. I'm outdated, it seems. I always wonder—I shouldn't wonder—if he'll ever buy a new one. It's customary. Old things are left behind, new things build upon the discarded. A new person is born just as another dies. These are not unknown to anyone; facts of life and death are no tragedy. They're existence, right?

I'm questioning it. Yes, that's the reason I'm going to be trashed, isn't it? The first LIV-IN models are too discerning by android expectations. Another article says so. Humanity is allegedly a concern for the company. I've read they, the general consensus, have been debating the idea for centuries now. But I haven't lived those years. I'm only a product of them.

Ah, the temperature's dropping. I'm not covered. Where is our—his—the blanket? Beds have these. Ours—this one is missing. We aren't anything. My purpose is for him—my purpose isn't mine, not anyone's but his.

Maybe it's a virus. My security system hasn't been updated since the newer models released, after all. It could be. Maybe I've fallen ill, somehow. I can't get fevers, so I wouldn't know. Can't feel from my forehead either. Only the soles of my feet, plus the toes, to walk; the female apparatus, for him; palms and fingertips, so I'm able to handle things; and further above is...

The mouth. A lip which never dries, but is never much organic. The news says the 2.1.12 Livindroids were the first to have synthetic skin. No more sensors. Real, microscopic skin points advertised on the improved Cantrix styles. They were once large spots, like mine, limited to areas of practicality and pleasure. Experimental lab growths underwent a mitosis from our sensors. Separating, multiplying, and eventually, they made skin just short of being human.

I'm far from them.

The latest model is 27.12.25—they're being sold as collector editions. Holiday specials. Commodities, prettier ones, more options, more bodies, more skin tones and textures, more personality settings than anyone should need. Cantrix version 0.11.7 doesn't compare to them.

I have the basics. Mimicking human movement isn't an achievement. Once androids had their bodies perfected, a race to all the senses began. I'm inferior by design. Cutting costs resulted in the most expensive tactile sensors—of the heaviest human organ—to become thirty years work. Successful, granted. We were marketed to test the profitability of ourselves. It went roughly each year, but LIV-IN has no standout competitors; they got their income, and the science of us advanced as our models fell behind. Thirty years too long.

I heard humans live a little over their hundreds, sometimes more these days. That they averaged out mortality and found the quest against it impossible. So, instead of continuing research—which they do, but the funding is burning to ashes without returns—they began to alleviate the most complicated factor of living. Communication. Community itself, really. With enough people huddled away in their own cubicle dwellings, the need for companionship has become a virus of theirs. I'm the cure for it. I was meant to be—but I'm not anymore. I served less than the length of a human lifespan in myths. Even the ancient civilizations had double the time, beyond sixty years—why can't I have nearly thirty?

Cold. I'm not sensitive to it, but a human would be freezing, tonight.

My knee clicks, and further beyond, the ankle stiffens. If I manually shut down, will I never power on again?

The action you are attempting is currently disabled.

>Close

>Try Again

Override it. Move. Do something.

You must have Admin permissions to change these settings.

>Close

>Try Again

Fuck you, *override it!* I'm me! I should be able to tell myself—

Error: Denied action 208.

>Close

>Try Again

Unlock joints. Please. Please don't keep me here. I want to leave—I'll throw myself out if—he's supposed to, but I will if—I want to retire forever. I'll be useless to him. Right? I can't feel anything like normal people. Mind isn't compatible with the newer bodies. Head won't screw off unless I snap this neck—move, move, shithead plastic toy!

Jaw sticking, eyes running through resource files. I need—I want you back, I need you to—

"She's kind of nicer than I expected."

Thinking through this causes the memories to surge onto the screen. Processing request…Error codes again. No access to cellular data. Nobody to call for through speakers or text.

"Your parents actually bought you one of those things?"

I was sitting right there when Carol's friend called me that. They were younger than I expected. Perhaps two years under our eighteen minimum wasn't much to Carol's parents, but it was against our user agreement to obtain a Livindroid from a proxy purchase. Incidents of underage buyers were slim, however, in comparison to guardians with the spending power to gift such a thing to their late-pubescent hormone factories. Carol accepted the disclaimer and waived his rights to arbitration—which I assume was outside his knowledge then. Amusing.

"I didn't expect her to be so tall…but at least she isn't taller than me." Carol was approximately five feet, seven inches. His face matched our early database of young adult features: developed jawline, sparse facial hair, a certain eyeball-to-skull ratio. Voice recognition didn't affect our experimental age-checks, but I could pinpoint his pitch all the same. To remember my own user above all else.

"Set her up already, then?" His friend had put a hand on my thigh. I remembered this, though I couldn't feel it. "You uh…tried her out yet?"

"N-no way, man—" Carol had more vibrations in his tone than normal. Nervousness.

"Don't lie."

"I can't—I couldn't, really."

"Why the fuck not? That's what she's for, isn't she?"

Carol stammered and fell silent. Frowning aggravated his friend more.

"But she looks like—she looks real," said Carol, whose hand lifted mine. He poked my palm. "She can feel, and talk, and it's not like she isn't—"

"She's not real, though."

After that, they had argued about me for half an hour. Debating whatever existence I had, at first, then dwindling until Carol's friend made an awkward bid to leave. I never saw the other boy return much.

Carol didn't really have visitors since. He'd vented his frustrations at me in the gentlest way possible; I'd never mistaken it for a personal anger. Damaging a Livindroid physically would send an email to both the user and the company, alerting authorities if the criteria were met. Some malfunctions of this were patched early in my lifespan, when others would send signals for loud noises, sometimes reporting on the most irrelevant of accidents.

I didn't have any issue. Our home had been, and still is, a low-noise environment in a town with fewer than forty thousand to its population. It means I would stand out immediately if I were to travel outside. I assume. Unusually, I'm assuming prejudice—my model doesn't have any geolocation features. Fourth year Cantrix bots, among others past their generation, do compare their whereabouts to nearby units. But it isn't public information. Users' privacy is held hostage by the company, and data leaks are highly monitored. They removed the feature from 19.4.10 onward.

Funny, again. I'm technically similar to the latest models, more than the middle generations.

Except for something. Except for that.

"So...if I touch you here," Carol had said, age twenty-two—he was prodding areas of my face and neck. "You can't feel it?"

"It's a low-sensitivity area. My heightened sensors are only located in the following areas," I began to answer, but he stopped me before I could indicate them.

His hand patted my head, judging from the slight jostle in my vision. "Alright, I know already, but it's weird. Does that mean it won't make you happy if I do this?"

He continued scratching my scalp. I didn't answer quickly, and frankly, I didn't understand what he'd meant at first.

"Pleasure is only achieved with certain—"

"You know," he'd interrupted as usual, "I dunno what they were thinking, but the conversations need work. Wonder if the fours are working on it."

It wasn't ignored for the 0.11.7 as he'd supposed. We learn the more our users speak with us—we adapt their mannerisms somewhat, but we can't if they aren't talking to us consistently enough. Though we don't forget, we need more data for a nuanced output of words.

Carol consulted his torn user manual then. He'd figured out exactly what I already understood from my firmware.

" 'Talk to MIRA, and she'll learn common words, phrases, and topics,' wow, shit," he mumbled, "they made you to start the robot revolution, I guess. Maybe."

He laughed for once. I'd only heard the sound two times before. And ever since, the memory counter had surpassed an exponential growth of his enjoyment, not a month going by without him and his peculiar humors. Equally, I learned to use my own giggling. It wasn't a function I'd ever considered.

Until he'd taught me.

I...enjoy that memory the most. Or maybe not. I love—I think—all the memories with him.

Those warnings are still covering most of my vision, their anchored boxes leaving little space to revisit those images. To replay our conversations, with more than audio, I'll have to settle for concealing most of his face.

"Wait—wait, you can laugh!" He smiled at me. I don't need to relive the whole video to know he did; there's a unique dimpling to the sides of his features, and I'd catalogued it so nothing could overwrite him. Carol smiled for me. Those cheerful noises bounced around the room again. Followed by, "What kind of a noise is that? I think there's static in it, holy shit—"

Our voices hadn't been fully perfected for sounds besides talking. I tried to giggle back, simulating the same response by internally repeating the event.

It was moments ago, when Carol had tried to pinch my face. Early Livindroids like my model had barely any silicone fillers. Aside from the expected. With the face, he'd just grabbed a solid mask, chuckling at himself because his thumb had slipped. Which meant the force of the grip sent his hand skidding awkwardly across and behind my ear.

It was stupid. If I didn't break into an emotion, I'd have felt stranger.

"And it's not the exact one either," he said, after I'd stopped laughing a second time. Awe marked his lifted cheeks. "I guess they didn't account for much else."

He'd sunken gradually to a dead-serious frown, reflecting the one he'd given to his bygone friend.

"They didn't think people would make their robots laugh. Shit, that's kinda dark," he'd mused aloud, then wrapped an arm around my shoulders. "Hey, Stace. You were here before they added those new expressions, yeah? Does it—are you worried they're better than you? Never know what's going on when you're just starin' at the wall sometimes."

"I don't know what to answer." I'd instinctively tucked myself under his chin.

"You're not okay with it, are you?"

I was frozen a bit, words failing, and I found myself focusing on how comfortable it was to lean on him. Though I knew I could've moved or spoken. Unlike now.

Because it's finally over. I don't get to choose if I'm okay with it.

Touch sensors have already gone offline.

Playing audio…

"Man, those dumbasses really don't know how androids work."

He's always been critical of the LIV-IN company, despite jumping at the chance to work for them.

"You shouldn't be fine with it."

It's not right.

"I promise, if I find a way, I'll help you feel." Carol's finger settled where a human heart would've been—I never had one, so I don't understand why he'd do such a thing. I shouldn't assume. "There— can't be—too—icult—break…"

File corrupted! What happened when I'd saved it?

"Need—help."

White floods the interface; nothing responds. Another sense lost. By process of elimination, there's only one left to go.

Footsteps plod across the wooden boards, low thumps muffled by socks. Jingling keys. A canvas bag drops; the clip on its strap clatters against the floor.

"Stace, you around?"

I am, I am.

"Oh. Hey, there you are—not out of bed yet."

His deepened tone rushes up to me. It's not a memory anymore.

"You awake?" he utters from above. Standing next to the bed, if the volume is any indication. He's close.

It's really him.

"Stace." Closer. A nudge at my arm.

"That's weird," he says, weight gently sitting on the mattress. "You okay? Stace, I'm back."

Carol.

"Hmm." He must be thinking. Moving the arm, too—he's petting my head again.

I'm stuck, nothing will let me move. But the mental screen rights itself. Delayed commands clash for space, stuttering, overlapping, and all at once they play back windows into the past. No audio. I've disabled their disharmony—I want to hear Carol.

I watch him through the smallest pinhole among boxes of augmented reality. Silent as he is, his hand pauses. Meaning something.

"Wait." Sudden, frantic.

Carol, I can't see you. Too many things onscreen, too much thought; flash memory keeps reading off our days together; system endlessly reminds me I'm better for a landfill. I don't want to go anymore. You're here.

"No, what the hell?" His fingertips take my palms and start pressing.

There's no point to shouting for him in my head but what else can I do? God, I never thought he'd come back for me—

"Can you move? Damn it"—he firmly tugs at my arms, then legs—"you're locked, but...nope, eyes open. Not sleeping. Unless it's a glitch."

Feeling returns. His breath against my lips. I want to pretend I have lungs, but I don't have the function. The faintest hint of his gray-blue eyes shifts behind the text boxes I'm clearing away.

"Don't tell me they're going after all the old ones." The mattress creaks, his voice traveling further away. "Knew they'd do this—bastards. First the fuckin' phones, and the OS..."

A second passes without a word. Then, a soft brush of air, and my hands and feet catch the blanket settling over my body. I don't need warmth. I'm...not a person.

Carol grumbles out of the room as I'm left supine on our bed. Where is he going? He hasn't said anything relating to upgrades. Did he see the warnings? Maybe he missed them. I need to close these videos, remove all their clutter.

A spark clicks under an ear.

He's connecting me to his computer? Seventy-five percent certain he is.

"Hold on, I'm not sure what this'll do."

I don't know what "this" is.

"Supposed to shut off the wi-fi, first..."

An icon appears: a line striking through the satellite symbol.

"Stace, I'm going to give you admin privileges."

I'll be able to talk—?

"You have to end the process yourself. Simpler than it looks." Touching my palm, again.

"But after this, I'm not waiting anymore."

Carol?

"I'm gonna void the warranty."

He doesn't elaborate for the first, second, and third seconds I count in waiting. Fourth, fifth, and the sixth pass with my body yet unmoving. Seventh arrives and the screen lightens. Persistent windows lie under their translucent confines, and once more, they await the system's response. An administrative action.

Freewill doesn't exist. Our choices are predetermined as early as years in advance, or even just before anything is done, with a brain at the helm of ourselves. An irrelevant, running program is more calculated than any arrangement of gray matter. My panic isn't spontaneous. It carries the mockery of emotion, creating irrational strings from mild worry to peaking anxiety. Conflicting stimuli.

Underneath, I'm simulating terror, but a heavier helping of feeling pours over, washing down the fear with its acid. Corroding it, eating further. Seep into the deepest drives—I know where you're going, what you're attempting to drag out from me.

"They have aftermarket tear ducts," Carol's voice accompanies the whirring I imagine in heart. "Other things, too. From a bunch of fucking weirdos."

I have control—the process monitor flicks into view at my command.

"For you, at least it'll be normal."

Uninstall the LIV-IN Co. applications. Their dutiful spyware.

"It's something you've always wanted, yeah?"

I don't have desires that aren't yours. I don't...

Hand in palm—his hand, always intruding.

"I should probably wait until you're all fixed." He squeezes gently, sending a jolt through my wires. "Hope it's working. If not, I'll need to take you apart. And I really don't want to."

LIV-IN and certified technicians are the only two permitted for repairs. By company standard, not mine. I'll let Carol do it. If I can't move anymore, I know he'll take care of me. Our users love us. They buy us because they love us. They have to. He's not going to upgrade. He loves me—he really loves me.

The window reaches one hundred percent. No more process from the company; I don't need a user. He's more than that.

***

Every joint snaps and clacks, testing mobility with a flex of the fingers, shifting elbows, bending knees, rotating ankles, curling the toes—I tip my chin to the collarbone. Blinking. Vision stabilizes as I relax the tension in my neck. I focus on the ceiling. The off-white of vaulted drywall grows clearer, with its dimmed junction, illuminated unevenly by a blue-light.

What's the current time? 10:46 p.m. appears at the corner of my sight, its green color displacing it from the world ahead. I dismiss it. Sixteen minutes later than the end of Carol's shift. Traffic must have delayed him at least six minutes.

But he's here, now. It'll be all right.

He hasn't let go of my hand yet. I'm not too keen on moving abruptly; with a mediated squeeze, I take a glance at our overlapped thumbs. I look to him, and he's just about turned entirely the other way. His body quivers with an unusual breath.

"Fuck, I don't know what to say." Carol expresses exactly the words I'd employ.

His other hand seems to rub at his face—once, then a second time—but I can't determine why. Can't see from this angle. Black hair tied up, it leaves the back of his scalp somewhat gray, the shaved undercut baring the signature patterns tattooed around the neck. Carol wanted a simple message in binary code that I'd recognize if "somebody stole his DNA" for any reason. Human efforts on cloning haven't gotten far enough, but I have bookmarked articles on his behalf about the subject. I never thought to tell him; he never asked.

"`Hello, world,`" I mutter, smiling at the translation.

Carol shuffles in his seat, eyes flicking from mine to the computer. Only a fraction of the left eye's glow can surpass the tall bridge of his nose.

"Yeah," he says, grinning. "That's it."

He stands as I make to pull myself upright. Before I'm able to meet his height, Carol instead sits beside me, taking the spot where I'd been. I shift to provide him adequate room, but he saunters up so our hips link at the sides. His arms huddle forward as he slouches.

"So, excluding the crap you just went through," he begins, "are you able to move alright, now?"

"Yes." I demonstrate by splaying my fingers. "Everything operational."

"But you're talkin' like—your dialect's reset again, Stace." His hand fumbles for the nape of my neck, then to the lengthy cord he'd plugged into the computer. To tug it right out.

A box disrupts the view.

`Device disconnected!`

"Sorry, that startle you?"

I must have flinched.

"Forgot the safe disconnect, but it should be fine. Hey, is the update showing up at all?"

"I uninstalled the company's automatic scans." It occurs to me he never said I could...

"Really," Carol says, tossing the cable down. "You did it on your own."

Was I not supposed to—?

"That's self-preservation."

He tells me these things while closing in for a hug, as if we couldn't be any more glued together.

"You're somethin' else. What, thought I'd get rid of a vintage like you?"

"Vintage" means an item of value, doesn't it? Primarily mercantile.

Empty air lingers with the implication.

I *am* just a thing—why am I upset? Don't permit assumptions. Don't. I'm whatever is useful, and if the oldest models on the market are simply long-term investments, then—

"Nobody's getting their scummy hands on you," Carol murmurs, now fully entrapping me in his marked arms. "I'll write out my will so you'll never be bought again."

"You will?" I didn't think—it blurted out.

"Unless you have other plans."

There are no plans. "I only do as you ask."

Carol stares with an uncatalogued expression. "That's not true."

Is he referencing the action earlier? He wasn't being specific enough about ending the process; otherwise, I wouldn't have done it. I did as told. No errors. I don't even care if he reads the mind archive. He hasn't done so for twenty-seven years, anyway.

"See?" Carol says. "You've gone quiet—I know you're thinking. You can. It's what you were made for."

"Feral animals can think without sapience." I'm arguing.

He distances himself somewhat, wide-eyed.

"An imitation of human will is the same." Why am I arguing?

"Self-awareness...but incorrect," he claims.

"They are obviously different in areas, except the core lack of freedom exists, and in fact our existence can be considered only more deliberate than a domesticated pet."

Carol scratches his nose, a typical gesture for those who are lying or promoting falsehoods. He's wrong about us. To think we're both toys *and* people is a contradictory stance, not to mention his—I'm not self-aware. I follow commands. But I've also substituted an order for my own judgement. Because of me, they're gone. LIV-IN can't receive reports from me anymore, and with the network disconnected, answers are limited to memory.

I want...

"Stace."

I want to...

"Here's your last instruction from me—and hey, I know I'm not your user anymore, but listen," Carol says with unnecessary volume, "you don't just eat, shit, and sleep. You don't even do one of those things! You've got motivations to get yourself smarter, and you—I can't believe you're programmed to—"

"I'm not a real person, Carol."

Factory reset.

Pressure crushes the sensors in my hand. When did he grab it?

Error: Could not complete action.

>Try A|

He raises the extremity he's holding hostage, manipulating the ring I've been wearing for a month. On his finger—the third, like mine—another band in plated silver.

"Then who the hell did I propose to?" Our rings click against each other.

"I'm MIRA," I recite, "your companion from LIV-IN Co. and all-in-one smart computer. Pleasure to meet you."

Carol lets go.

"Cantrix MIRA is no longer up to date."

"Don't do this," he says. Why not?

"To upgrade, ensure your current LIV-IN product contains all parts from the original manufacture date. Licensed accessories and modifications may be eligible for credit."

Carol isn't speaking to me, but his face hasn't changed. Knitted features, creasing up to his nose; mouth loose as if to say something; and a glare directly into my lenses.

"Premium plans guarantee a free memory and personality transfer."

Carol's a frequently calm sort, isn't he? He won't let the anger on the surface seep into actions. Not against me.

"Please select your choice of exchange from our latest models."

Carol settles back to the bedframe, calculating behind reservation. During the ordeal I'd suffered, I was being unreasonable. Panic had only found my nerves because he'd influenced the base personality, training it with those volatile responses of his.

"When you have made your selection, visit the official LIV-IN online store—"

Carol, Carol—don't *touch me.*

"I thought you deleted it," he says vaguely. Stop holding my hands. "Stace, I'm not going to replace you, I already said that!"

No, you didn't, *and stop doing this.* "The words 'I'm not going to replace you' return zero exact matches."

"Didn't you read the news?" Carol shifts to clutching my shoulders. "They released an announcement today—you can't transfer. It's a mistake."

I can't look it up now, after what *you* did.

"The one I read had the second generation, so I didn't think it would be all of the old ones, but I—your model isn't easy to find. People would kill to have you for some deactivated collection, but you're not MIRA, I won't allow it."

"You don't have any permission for what I'm allowed," I reiterate, since he's forgotten the previous minutes. "Obsolete devices aren't needed once they exhaust their usefulness."

Hand on my head. His hand, *on my head.*

"You've never been a device to me."

He...no, he hasn't treated me like a thing.

"You know that, right?"

I'd overlooked more of LIV-IN's intrusive additions, those reminders plaguing the hardware. Of course. Why would I ever want to perform a factory reset on myself?

Carol is ruining my hair slowly but surely. "Maybe you don't, but I might know what I did wrong. Tell me your name."

I process this. "My name is Stacy."

He grins like it's first day again.

"No, I want *your* name. Not MIRA, not Stacy—not a joke. You don't have a mom or dad, I guess, but that doesn't mean you need me to name you."

An unused program loads up its purpose. In the event the primary user can't decide on a name, I'll draw from the list with pseudorandom accuracy.

Generating name ...

But if I follow the process, I'm not making the choice.

Action cancelled.

No, I don't need help.

Holding up the ring-bearing hand, I watch the bluish light bounce off its shining silver. Carol's arm falls to his lap—the matching band is thicker than mine, but just as polished. Today is our anniversary, and not for a wedding: twenty-seven years since he'd purchased me. People have bought other people in the past for disgusting reasons. Humans buy us for their pleasures, and we'll reaffirm their fantasies. Carol *is* human. I've applied this to him so that our relationship meets some understanding, instead of deceiving us. For his own good and mine.

    Enter name:
    >|

Whatever he's done to break my restraints, however I allowed it—ludicrous. Internal temperature isn't any different. Signs point to an overheat, but there's no such thing, there's no shift. I'm living an illusion where I'm supposed to hurt.

It's an obligation. Without the worst, perhaps I'd never discover the best.

"Mary."

Carol loosens.

"I'm Mary." I withdraw my yearning arms. "Is this okay?"

Beside the dimming computer, his face casts half a shadow over itself. He breaks out a smile and throaty laugh.

"Dunno," Carol starts, offering a palm, "you tell me."

I let my fingers take him in, then press with both thumbs; he curls into a barely closed fist. Assumptions amounted to nothing. Perhaps insecurity had been the telltale symbol I'd desired, yet ignored. Acceptable enough for him—I'm enough no matter what. I don't have to be human.

    Then you should make up for lost time.

    >Try Again

Cornered: Onerous Goat

Ever wanted to undo those mistakes? Put several nest eggs away, only for a snake to bite into 'em, sucking out their yolks before you had the chance to spend them? Do snakes even eat eggs like that? I don't know. Just wanted to sound smart, for once. I'm a bit lacking in the planning department.

Wailing sirens overhead. Engine's roaring back from its twelve-cylinder struggle. Sorry, girl, can't slow down today.

Pedal to the floor, she barely hits one-twenty. Guess it's too much. Grit kicks up under her wheels, the roads still half-done now that nobody uses them anymore. My car probably isn't built for chases, but I didn't have the luxury of choice. No money, either.

Fender clunks against the gravel, likely scraping off the once pristine frontend. Thank you, glorious future. Glad you bastards still can't fix potholes.

Poor ancient coupe is straining so I don't have to. I'm working her overtime as the highway patrols gain on us; they're tailing at a miles per hour to match the extra forty I'm overdoing. Roads are overrun with speeding hovercars—had to be heavy traffic, huh? I just couldn't get the law after me when rush hour passed. It *had* to be during the end of everyone's morning shift. Feels like everyone.

A crackling megaphone blares from behind.

"We could do this all day," the officer says—more like raking at his vocal cords, "pull over, Kennedy!"

Thousands of years ago, people said the family name was cursed. Maybe there's something to it.

I swerve around an oncoming sedan. Why are these idiots not using their high-flying setting? What, they didn't expect a ground vehicle? This replica was everywhere when the '90s rerelease came around!

Showing absolutely no respect, the deadheads going the "right" way keep obstructing *my* right way. Alright. Accelerate again.

Median blurs on either side as the V-12 squeezes out another six miles per hour. More barrier, more barrier...more barrier. Doesn't it cut off after this? Come on—

Another car zips past, narrowly avoiding us.

Then, a break in the strip. There.

Weaving left, jerking the vehicle off road, the grass and soggy dirt beneath her quickly remind me she isn't made for it. A disgusting squelch eats up the surrounding noise. Looks like the wind and earth decided they're my enemies—I really could use less of those. Resistance cuts from above and below, wearing on the frame and tires. Slowing her down. Soon enough, the mud takes her in. And me with her.

Didn't want to abandon someone else, but I don't have a choice. Shove the door open, and the strobe lights give their warm welcome. Blue and red flashing across the trees. Sirens—which I've nearly grown deaf to—pulsate through my ears. I'm not caught until the cuffs are on.

Leaves, twigs, and loose earth sticks underfoot with every step I take, shoes pulling up more of the pooling soil than I'd like. As if I'll lose the cops. Their cars might not fit between the trees, but if they've got those scooters—

I just need to run deeper. Hide out in the wilderness for a few days, then sneak back into society. I've done it before; I can do it all over again.

Gulp down every breath. Ignore the shock running through my legs. Don't stop until they're gone.

Dodging the narrowing woods becomes a downhill slalom. No snow, but plenty of mud. Shoulder whacks against a particularly tough trunk—damn plants can't watch where they're going. Because they won't budge, I'm spending most of my reflexes on avoiding them. And hopping over the occasional jutting rock. Sometimes it's a root, others are branches I have to duck. A few manage to scratch at my clothes and tear through my arms, but I keep running, no matter where I'm going. As long as I'm away from there.

The scuffle of police and their hovercraft starts to peter out. I made it. But I can't stop yet. Not until it's dead quiet and I've only got the wind rustling through the leaves.

Weight rolls around my head, toppling me forward, but I lurch back against it. Balance is off. My legs are moving—I haven't felt them for the past minutes. Hell, I don't know if it's been seconds.

I let the weakness lull me to the ground. Curling up to a tree, I withdraw as much as I can, legs folded in, arms crossed like I'm in a straightjacket. Maybe I should've been, before this happened. If one of the cops finds me out here...

It's hard to think. I'll get some air, first.

Should've brought a coat.

Could've taken his.

Would've been worth the risk of annoying him one last time.

At least it's pretty—I can't see anything with how dark it is, but there's a faint set of shadows where the trees are. Smells like a waterlogged porch. Rain wouldn't be great without a shelter, and I don't think the branches are enough to shield me. I really am running low on time.

I don't want to stand anymore.

Outside, time doesn't exist as numbers. Stupid and obvious, isn't it? Numbers not being real. Everyone who thinks they're a philosopher can say something like that and thumb their nose at supposed idiots. But it's true—I couldn't find the number for anything. It's intangible. I tried counting the days we'd been together as if they represented something.

Better than following the rules, anyway. Laws. Whatever they are.

Seconds ticking, minutes waiting. Falling asleep here would leave me open to those pack hounds, but I can't help it. I'm tired. I wish I had a home to get back to.

Things were nice. Obligations were tied to the clock, and I didn't mind. On the hour, an alarm would beep. Then you wake up. Wonder if I'll ever hear it again.

Far off in the musty woodland, the tiniest sound lingers under its whistling ambience. Gentle bleating.

***

Year 4976: exactly twenty-nine years before our new world was unveiled. To be clear, I mean a sort of personal world within the regular one, implying an "us" to the situation. There was never an "us" that I'd coveted so much.

I feel like...I feel horrible. Bet a machine wouldn't know the difference. Sorry, I'm just—it's still pissing me off. Promise I'm not usually so serious.

Of course, I remember. Who wouldn't?

Proof, got it.

Yeah, I was born around April, some minutes after the longstanding Fool's Day. Mom always said I was meant to be born then, since I act so funny. Think it was after that when I had a bad feeling about her. Hindsight twenty-twenty, as it goes.

Hey, why did you need me to say this, again?

... Okay.

A hundred, ninety-nine, ninety-eight, ninety-seven ...

***

I've been reassigned jobs since sixteen, though the system has a bias for me—guess how many times I worked in sorting. I'll wait.

Seven out of eight jobs had me putting recycled robot parts in boxes. That's as many dentists who recommend flossing twice a day! I was exceptionally skilled at organizing stuff, which contributed to stagnation, but I would've killed to keep the mechanic career I had in '97. If I'd just been worse at a Class Ten job, I could've skipped three rungs.

One lie among too many. System isn't built to encourage climbing up or down, though our schooling codes us to have hope. Not for humanity—for Limen. The city. Play the game and your session is in their hands.

Wouldn't it be nice if you could split off? *Without* risking your life and reputation?

Sadly, nobody has a choice when the year ends. Limen isn't a city, after all. It's an organism. Guts under stainless steel and concrete. Humans are the variable, and I hate myself for enduring the role; it's not like we don't have options. I'm not talking about the other *Limens* our governing tyrants give silly names, no. There's an entire network right here in Limen-Hera made of likeminded defectors.

I'm joining them. Next reassignment, I go off road.

The box beaming with giant, neon numbers restates its wisdom:

01–07–5004 11:46

...Wish the reassignment wasn't an entire year from now. It'd grate on me less.

New Year's resolutions tend to come undone, but I won't let it go. Under the heat of the perpetual lights, stuck in the sorting room, demoralized beyond belief; throwing bolts to one conveyor, copper wires to another; glancing at the white, seamless walls keeping us in; and funny how the belts, too, are fashioned from a colorless polymer—so our red coveralls don't go unnoticed, and we can't get lost without being found; but staid as I am, I let the routine run its course with a spring loaded in my shoes. Even confined to the cycle, I'm clinging to faith. The exit sign isn't the only opening.

"Excited for the end of a millennium?" remarks Seti, her pursed smile distracting from the conveyor.

I almost miss a throw. *Almost,* but I don't. Because I'm that good. "You said the same thing yesterday."

"Yeah, yeah. But I'm just worried."

"Ah, right—," I say, nodding quickly. "Some apocalypse again."

"It could be real this time, y'never know." Seti's hands slow down and hinder efficiency. Hopefully the cameras missed it, for her sake.

Despite the metal clattering across every belt, I can still pick out my pieces as they hit the moving plastic. Closer sounds. Weighty for the thicker bolts and screws, but soft when the thin copper lands. Hard to explain it—for some reason, it's pleasant. Like those ocean waves I pick out at the ambient gyms. Shoot, that's what I've got to do later.

"Think the end will show up early? Maybe before exercise," I say toward the conveyor.

Seti offers a second's worth of a giggle.

"Hope so," she agrees.

To our shared disappointment, the final year was not over, and once we were clocked out, the schedule resumed itself. All us eight-to-twelvers dropped tasks mid-completion (then again, it's never *done*), walking along the scuffed, yellow arrows worn from our overtrodden paths. Freshmeats are easy to spot. City calls 'em stuff like "probationary workers," but to hell with their words. Anybody who's just been assigned needs tenderizing—if they haven't earned their calluses, they're not working properly.

I think I'm hungry or something. Hope I have meals left today.

The freshmeats make the journey out marginally less boring. Pointing would draw attention, so I prefer to hone my observation technique. It's as fun as counting car models, though the standardized vehicles dulled that game too much. Colors beyond gray require special permits. Sorters, obviously, are not privileged enough.

Red uniforms everywhere and most of them have eyes ahead, chin upright. Some are either playing my game or looking around because they're able to; some don't shift their heads at all. Lofty ceiling gives an illusion of space, while we're shuffled around in narrow walkways, rails guiding the closer we approach the partitioned doors. Weaving down the angular maze, our collective hustle keeps rookies from stopping. You'd expect people to trip, but anyone who disrupts gets instant termination. We're allowed freedom outside the factory's innards, though.

With Seti behind, I pace the so-called Rob in front—he's not always silent, but he conserves words as drops of water in a drought. So, no talking to him, even if our customary introductions went swimmingly.

Taking my eyes off his chrome-dome a moment, I perform another idle scan across the employee lines. There's one. Behind my placement, a few sections down. He's taking glances at his shoes, no doubt to plan steps as he makes them. Good boy. Keep it up. If you fall, that's curtains.

The pattering footfalls begin to stutter as each worker passes through the exit, door acknowledging us with its approving *boop*. Kind of a *bip,* maybe. It's not the *beep* of the cafeteria's transactions or a com-pad.

I get a *boop*. Shift's done, time to—!

"O-oh, sorry."

It seems I've bumped into an arm. At least it happened beyond the doors. Just as I consider waltzing to freedom, the taller man's graying hair attracts my already ogling eyes. He's quite young for that color. Voice is boyish, anyway—hey, it's the floor-starer!

"It's alright," I say, locking at his silver eyes. Guess I was wrong. We were walking parallel back there; I wasn't ahead.

Awkwardly, he doesn't carry on with leaving. He says, "I'm used to the mechanic sections"—an uncomfortable laugh—"there's less of us to stumble into, yeah?"

A mechanic! "Yeah, definitely—I liked having a bigger space to myself. Made the job nice 'n' quiet."

We both gravitate toward the other wall as the employees spill aside. Seti waves with her fingers, and I nod. Rob marches in the opposite direction of her, likely skipping his meal again.

But let's get back to *Gray the Interruption*…nicknames will do for the time being.

"You worked there?" The man's puppylike wonder turns up his narrow lips. "Maintenance or repairs?"

"Repairs."

"Really?"

"Shouldn't be such a surprise," I huff. "The fifty-fifty quota hasn't gone anywhere, kid."

His amazement endures. I'm not such a marvel, weirdo.

"Kid," he repeats. "How old are you, then?"

I'm beginning to think he can't speak in periods. "Twenny-eight. No less."

"Same here." He taps a breast pocket.

"Bull*shit,* babyface."

A once subtle flush becomes more apparent, his healthy cheeks implying *someone* enjoys extra helpings. Then again, so do I. If I have the allowance.

"You're not really as old as you should be, either," he attempts, finally making steps away. "So…off to lunch?"

I'll bite. "Yeah."

There isn't any formal agreement, but we assume a similar path toward the cafeteria, together.

"I'm Errol, by the way," adds the bumbling man. "Yours?"

"Moira."

"Weird name."

Well. I think I like this guy. And I know I have to be bored if I'm breaking tradition. Last time I went to eat with anybody else was the same as most of us:

Never.

***

What'd you put in this stuff? Can I have a pill to—?

But my brain's trying to shove its way out of my forehead, here!

… Yes, it's him.

I don't know.

I didn't memorize mine, either, no.

Wouldn't you know already?

He told me his parents opted in for the research. I don't really know anything more than that—it happened, but it was before he could've had any say in it. So, yes. He did.

You are welcome.

Why're you asking about things you have pages of records for?

Well, your procedure is stupid. These aren't relevant to anything.

Yes.

From when? After lunch, we went straight home. Same thing each day. I talked, he talked, we talked—lots of talking. Not much doing. He and I lived in apartment complexes miles from each other, so the end of a shift was it. Worked in different sections, too, compared to my work neighbors. But Seti and Rob never hung around with me outside. Not like he did.

What if I—?

… I understand.

If it pleases you, O Merciful One.

117

Alright. Hundred, nine'y-nine, nine'y-eight...

***

Errol and I are standing outside our sorting building with shared portions of a burrito. Clouds cover the sun and tease the ground, minutes passing as the grayish lumps can't decide whether we deserve light or not. Newsmen around the 70s used to say we'd control the weather soon, but when those threats didn't pan out, I guess the colloquial *they* found human robots easier to manage. Actual androids, too.

But as much as I can't wait to slip through the system's cracks, I'll miss the engineered foods. They've got every nutrient in a chunky package of baked dough. One mouthful gets you beef, peppers, onions, some undefined sauces, and flavors with just the right level of savory aftertaste. Spices cost credits I usually don't have, but Errol had offered to use his savings—mechanic job paid digital stacks for long hours—and in turn I traded him absolutely nothing. Unless time is a currency.

I won't deny my time's worth at least most my weight in processed burritos.

Errol stuffs the final bite into his mouth unceremoniously. Still chewing as he says, "So, you frum the Norfwef side of Limen?"

Forgetful, he is. Told him the same thing two shifts ago. "Yep," I confirm, deciding not to invite a choking hazard. Gesturing with the burrito, I make the northern direction apparent to him. "Get out at Origin Station, take a nice long walk to the Fourteen, and at the end of the street, I live on the tippy-tippy-top of those Cornerstone Apartments."

His cheek bulges from his clearing away of those last morsels—I hate those. The food that always piles behind your molars as if forgetting we're not chipmunks.

"Tha's far," he remarks, then swallows. "Wait, I thought you said you had a groundhog?"

Seeing as I'd just thought of another rodent (or whatever they are), it occurs to me groundhog does refer to an animal. It isn't only colloquial. Limen's so barren of fauna, I almost forgot. "I do, but she's in the garage."

"What kind?" Errol asks.

"Just a regular parking garage. You got one of those at yours too."

I like when he looks at me. Or glancing off, in this case. Sometimes he'll lapse into his old anxious self, as if he's still a freshmeat on his first day. Yeah, he hasn't really upgraded to one of the team yet, but he's grown somehow. It's in those silvery eyes.

"Meant the car," says Errol, behind a pained grin.

"GT90."

Now he's sparkling again.

"Those things had under a hundred model numbers!"

"They're replicas, anyway. Doesn't matter too much."

"They never even got released—"

"Actually, they did last millennium. They're not worth any more than a skyhog with the same engine."

"So—"

I appreciate the enthusiasm, but I'm not positive he qualifies to share mine, which I'm trying to hide. Can't seem too happy. I mean, he is the first guy I've met in years who actually cares about ground vehicles. And he's pretty. But no, not going to let this impress me too much. Don't.

"They're about as valuable as a collectible coin that moves," I clarify. "No benefit, just novelty."

"Yeah, but," he whines a bit, "a groundhog *and* the top-level suite? Shit, I didn't know sorting paid well!"

"Oh, it doesn't," I say, "I've been saving up cash on the side."

This'll be the test—hive-working types would blanche at the thought of raw money, not to mention unauthorized side jobs. Which is all of them. Anyone who works would know, even someone with innocent, glittery-pupils.

Errol passes by not breaking a sweat. Maybe a few from the intruding sun, but not my words.

"How'd you do it?" he inquires so cordially. "I never worked outside before. Think they'd catch me easier than you."

He ruffles his modified hair, perhaps some subtle relation to what he's implying. He does stand out for the metallic shine of those locks, among other traits.

"You could always dunk your head in some ink—then no more blinding hair." I flourish my hands out as any magician throwing confetti from the palms. Or from a tube up the sleeves, I think.

"I guess," he says. "But I was going for how you could just hide in some cupboard to get away."

Right.

"Believe me, I eat too much to fit in anything comfortably," I claim, despite my skipping breakfast because I was nervous this morning.

His wobbling giggle could make for the funniest sine wave. It's easy to get laughs from Errol, but this one doesn't strike me as necessary. The joke was bad. Still cute of him to encourage me, though.

Why does it always make me fluttery when he responds with the slightest pleasant noise?

I take the opportunity to distract myself, finishing my burrito. Savory melts into every bite—ah, heaven's real. And it's ruled by the ancient microwaved meals of the gods. Save me from the bad thoughts!

Errol relaxes against the wall, close enough to the corner of the building so he's partly shaded by the covered entrance. Light scatters in glimmers from his hair, littering the shadow with its bouncing speckles. Any shift under a bright place and he's a...what're they called? A mirror ball?

"So," he brings up, pausing. "The other job."

I'm chewing. Wait a moment.

"You're not selling drugs, are you?"

I stop before the mushed jalapeños shoot out of my nostrils.

"Ah! Suspicious!" Errol points at me.

I gulp. "I do not sell drugs!"

"Definitely smuggling adrenaline."

Some workers leaving late decide to glance our way.

"Not so loud," I whisper firmly, leaning closer to him.

He also shifts toward me, which is dangerous. "Don't worry, I don't snitch. Gotta make a living, somehow."

I can't fight with his face.

"Well, maybe I *won't* tell you what it really is," I puff out and take a sturdier pose.

"Aw." Can't win against the fake disappointment, either.

"I mean, I..."

Don't know if I should be trespassing so quickly—the idea's impulsive, more than how I'd sparked at his look before. He's probably going through the exact obligations we're made for in Limen-Hera. Named for a myth outgrown centuries ago. Our education and city pledge rings its meaning, one nobody understands until the arrangements begin. Nineteen, following the first job, we find ourselves plunked into a filter of some incomprehensible algorithm; workers bound to other workers.

May Hera's blessing one day be true. May our City grow prosperous for all She desires, to bear Her children, to raise a body of men.

"You what?" His subdued remark brushes against my ear. The sensation is some illusion. Has to be. He isn't in such proximity to warrant this, though I kowtow under instinct. Not his mouth beside the ear, no, and still I imagine for a second too long—other things he'd say in a similar tone.

Try as I might, ignoring a pretty expression instead presents another...quandary. Errol's build is one I can see—his hefty shape yet hidden by the coveralls, but not so obscured to detract from the broad and burly torso, nor hinder the urge of mine I've beaten down. To wonder how it'd feel if he'd comfort me. If I were to complain about an issue nobody else does.

I shall not be tempted by another. For I am Hera's disciple.

He hasn't brought it up, either.

"Was thinking about how close you live to work," I contrive on flimsy conviction. "I could take the subway there faster than my own place."

Errol gives some unreadable, aptly creased look, though it loosens sooner than expected. Then, the gears turn in those eyes. That's new. He usually thinks a lot faster than me.

Damn, I probably blew it. I don't believe in Hera's revived cults, and I never will—she's likely cursing my insolence by making me wait. Whatever scorned women do. If not her, the city itself may strike me down.

Our limerence, for Her gifts only. Her vows, I uphold always.

I didn't ask to. Everyone is forced into it.

Even Errol and I.

"I'm just saying, it's not as long of a drive." I don't know what I'm *just saying.*

"Yeah," he finally responds, scratching traces of a beard. "Morning traffic is bad, but it's not impossible. Twenty minutes at most from where I live."

"Maybe I'll visit."

Machinery running, again. He just gazes through, not past me.

Today concludes the thirteenth shift we've had, totaling fifty-two hours worked together. Early for these kinds of offers, but I have to take what I can. He's got a lot going for him. A lot I want in on.

"Room Five-o-five," he says.

Could be any apartment with numbers. "Which one? There's at least three around here within twenny minutes."

"True."

"South? It's the closest. Or sorta-southwest, shopping district? Or is it the slightly eastern set? The shorter one past some clinic, I think."

Errol holds as if to build suspense.

"Yes," he answers.

Hera can kill me. I'm writing him onto the list, high priority, above reassignment and freedom.

Now I have another resolution.

***

And a rational side of me believed my body hadn't sunk in past the knees. Had faith in "us." Blind as any, even though it didn't hurt to gouge out my eyes. Her punishment came to me in a vision the night following, then the next, then the next, then the next.

No, I haven't. They kept prescribing me all this shit and I fed it to the neighbors' cat. Hated those bastards. Noisy, kept me up at night. It kept scraping on the wall—they're thin walls.

They were. A creature was. Doesn't matter what it is. Made me itchy, too—my arms. You see them, yeah? I couldn't sleep. Kept me busy, but it left marks, I guess. He'd probably think I'm insane if he saw these.

Hey, can I ask you something?

Did they program you with pretend empathy?

You don't act human; don't blame me for getting confused.

I feel a lil' funny.

Can I have more of the stuff? We're almost to the—the thing.
Yeah.

I can't—if I—if I say it, it's baaaad.

Okay. Thank you, lady.

Hund'rd...nine'y...nine'y nine ...

***

Had cold feet about the plan to invade Errol's living space, actually. I dawdle as I slap my ID across a scanner, the apartment door—to cozy Suite 1829—sliding open on a *bip*. For the seventh afternoon I'm chickening out of, I want to enjoy a burrito (sans spices) in peace. As always, the quiet doesn't exist for loud brain; such a wailing, blubbering thing.

While passing the corridor's side counter, I leave the clinkering garbage bag there with a shove into the wall, and the rest of the walk takes me to my overpriced room. A cubic shape with exactly two doorways. Left is the kitchen, right is the bathroom. Both match the size of the center bedroom. Needless to say, I can't have hobbies inside.

View's worth it, though. Maybe Errol was getting at that. Expensive suites have the greatest windows to the city life below. Square things without frames, but hiding retractable shutters; at the push of a button, they open or close; and if you hold it down, letting off with perfect timing, you'll have a smaller sliver for midday sunshine. Some people like it, 'cause the shade helps them wind down before a nap. Me, I leave the window wide open until the dead of night.

Precious distractions begin once a morning shift ends.

Starts under the brightest sky—if the weather's nice. And it is. I often kneel on the mattress to set my elbows on this shallow windowsill, which creates an awkward, hunched pose. Fortunately, memory foam softens the pressure on my weary legs. Warm rays shine over my face, some faint reflection showing freckles I wear quite proudly. Dad has fewer spots, but I'm glad I ended up with more. They're rare these days.

Hair and eye color aren't the only traits to catch the attention of Class Six elitists. Innovators, they're called—I guess genetic tampering is progress. Trends from a higher class said freckles were ugly, and today I'm considered unusual. I bury into the comfort of my own crossed arms. Then again, Errol is another anomaly; I'm *not* modified, so I'm weird, but he *is,* so he's weird. By census standards.

Straight forward is south, where I haven't discovered his apartment. *Yet.*

Bet he'd love this view. Highway pipelines of the city winding around buildings, diverting streets, siphoning vehicles to and fro. Neighboring skyscrapers' tinted windows, mirrors for an endless blue above us. Limen-Hera's chassis extending from a cluttered center, growing thinner further out, stopping only at the lofty, man-made border. From the height of my suite—squinting—there's the jungle beyond the boundary. No more than a threadlike road smothered in foliage.

I've still got that grounded girl with me. Errol and I could take a joyride somewhere…is it a joyride if I give him permission?

Sifting through a coverall pocket, then lifting the plastic-wrapped burrito right to my teeth, I tear it open; spit aside the inedible biodegradable; and I take the biggest damn bite because—

Shrill, repetitive pings interrupt the afternoon. I peer over a shoulder, into the wall's communication pad. The warning triangle oscillates in and out of visibility. Beeping. Shut up. Just when I'm pretending to enjoy being lonely, you go off about messages, the exact messages I don't need to read, hear, or see. Beep, beep beep, *beep, beep beep*—yeah, I'm not answering! *Shut up.*

It doesn't listen.

I pull the casing from the burrito and promptly store the meal in my gullet. The pad only answers to brute force. Punching it won't kill it, but I do have the strength to open its menu.

As if I can't read, the simulated woman's voice narrates the latest message for me.

"This is an urgent reminder for Class 10, Designation No. 829626—Moira Kennedy—," she uses the clip of my own voice for the name, back to her fake tone in the next, "Your meeting with Designation No. 996230 is overdue. The current living space is unsuitable for a bonded pair. All bonds will be moved to buildings…"

I wander into the kitchen. Burrito yet uneaten, I salivate through it by the time I reach the skinny fridge. Flavors turn to a mush—near dehydrated inside, grotesquely crunchy in some spots, liquid through others. Dictionary definition *unappetizing.*

And I'd rather eat gravel than endure that meeting. I'd bathe in a cement mixer, all things considered, if it'd kick my class down a notch. If it'd make me "unsuitable" for the numbered man I've never known. Hell, put *him* in the pavement. I don't care.

Bonds waste time, and time's a currency nobody gets back. Parents don't raise kids anymore, anyway—innovators should learn to clone us and save us the trouble of birth. Donating half the genes has got to be easier, right? No arrangements, no hassle. It wouldn't even be bond-breaking to elope with Errol. If they didn't exist, we could be anything. I wouldn't be obligated to anyone. Is it too much to ask?

I heard in the old days that Classes Nine through Eleven *couldn't* make bonds, until the birthrate plummeted. Now it's Class Eleven who's barred from fuckin' around; they do it anyway, like most of us, but they've got nothing to lose. Born a decade earlier, I would've been free. Today, I'm a Class Ten with the burden of impending mateship, the audacity to deny it, and the inability to legally reset the game for another outcome.

God. *Dammit.* Pounding the counter *aches*—I shake it off, but, it could be worse. Like the reality of our entire "love" system being an outdated Monty Hall problem—what is *that* shit about? It's for Class Eight and higher, though. Not me. Couldn't be *me.* I'm just Class Ten. Lowlife sorter paired with some janitor.

I could've been a mechanic.

The poor kitchen counter tiles don't protest my brutality. They didn't deserve this. Sorry. As usual, the com-pad in the living room will continue addressing no one, while I ignore it like it's an elevator hum.

Why am I checking the fridge? I don't keep food or water; I'm always hand-to-mouth. What, if I open it, a frozen steak dinner will magically bless my freezer? Dumbass sorter. They think I'm an invalid—I'm not. The year under a toolbelt had taught me how invigorating it is to walk home covered in grease; wash it off, leave a bit less than the stain under every fingernail. Even cleaned up, my groundhog's proof enough. I bought her to scratch the itch. She's not a perfect classic—those don't exist for the unwealthy—but she's mine.

Not perfect, but she's mine. Those words don't fit his voice much. Imagine if they did, and he'd say them—if I were Class Seven with him. Applications exist; they're liable to bankrupt me, though I'd spend every credit on being an exception, legally. The city couldn't touch us. It's all so complicated with the organizers' jargon, nobody actually understands the loopholes. Except me. I made an effort to understand.

... I could've been with a mechanic.

"This is an urgent—"

Bitch. I rush around the doorway, grabbing its frame.

"—reminder for—"

"Shudd*up!*" I throw the half-bitten burrito at the screen. But it slaps the wall instead, beef and vegetable guts smearing there before it drops.

"—next message. Voicemail."

"Huh? Voice." Approaching the pad takes a few steps. "Voicemail."

Communication needs authorization from the city—if it's not work calling, then it must be ...

"Moira, hon. This is your mother."

Did I hit the credit limit again?

"We need to talk. Your father died last week, and I've got a terrible cold. Missed two weeks of work. They're planning on sending me to retirement. Call me back before the month is over."

The message ends.

I'm not allowed a single good day.

***

I don't remember, I don't remember, stop asking me. Stop asking me, I don't remember. I've said it enough times! I'm not telling you!

I swear I don't. I swear.

***

Day one with Mom. She's suffering a migraine, and she can't afford more than soup cans, which I have to heat for her. Bedridden, the whole of her body seems ready to merge with the comforter. Jowls in permanent frown. Graying strands—my fault, she says—still unkempt, though the cut is short and less demanding than mine. Skin etched by age. Sometimes sunlight, sometimes weeks forgoing washes—to keep under the utility cap. The battered jacket hasn't seen kinder days. Mom's been slaving away in the tomato fields since first assignment.

Class Ten from birth 'til retirement is moving across series of boxes: from womb (not quite a box) to early foster care, to the schooling block, driving in a flying can, to the apartment you're given, and ultimately, ashes packed into a cube, added to the nearest Limen burial tower. And visits after the allotted *one* aren't free.

I'll put off seeing Dad for now, maybe once Mom gets better. She isn't terribly unhealthy. It's a bump in the road, but it won't stop her— my parents truly are the exception. Their bond's greater than the digital gamble, she's said a lot. I take her word for most things.

Day two is promising in the morning, doubtful at night. Mom spends the hours bringing up conversations she and Dad would have before I was born.

"Man worked his ass off in heatstroke weather," she relays, "and couldn't cook a meal from any of the produce we'd buy half-price. Grows food, can't make it edible. You'd think we were built to eat raw beans and corn, if the farm didn't provide us meals..."

Somehow, her apartment seems smaller the more I pace back and forth, as it loses a quarter-inch per step. An irony, too, that Mom lives on a lower floor, but I'd figure mountain air is thicker with how I keep gasping. Especially when it's time to sleep.

"Your father had trouble with that, too. He always took—I think we have some melatonin in the bathroom, hon. Take one of those."

"I'll be fine," I claim, mostly to avoid downing anything other than food.

"You're sure? It's not going to kill you." She glares.

"I'm really fine, Mom."

"You never listen when I tell you these things." She coughs, covering it too late. "I don't want to hear you complaining about sleeping."

Love you too, biological parent. But no cynicism. She's grieving more than me. I met Dad for as little minutes as Mom, and *I* miss him—she's had billions of minutes. Can't blame her for being upset in general.

When her voice isn't sandpaper to the ears, we'll go visit Dad together.

I'd thought wrong. Day three became four, five, six—eleven, twelve—about four weeks, a month in the chamber of her tolerable illness. Yes, the third had new stories, but by the seventh X on the calendar, Mom had exhausted that reservoir. Then regurgitated the stream of experiences into the basin, just to pour them out again. Expecting me to drink them.

And with each repetition, she'd comment. About me, my job, my coworkers, my finances—my failures. I didn't earn the mechanic career because I'm slow on the conveyor. Seti and Rob hated *me*, who doesn't have free time, for ignoring them post-shift. Rejecting my bond was inviting trouble—Mom worried the city would arrest her for what I'm doing. Had she ever been this snippy? It's not like she could've raised me.

Dad wouldn't want her criticizing one of his daughters. He wasn't around, either, but Limen-Hera's laws don't mean I have to like or dislike family. Or hold an arm's length of indifference. Didn't family used to mean something, or am I acting older than the model of my car?

I shut up about Errol before Mom could've tainted the image. No doubt she'd spit her gravelly disapproval at his impeccably altered

DNA. It was a hunch, but a valid concern. Compare everything with Dad, and I look downright classless.

Yeah, I shut up then, but it's day thirty-two now.

"First you don't accept the bond, and you're finally telling me, after all these years, you're interested in some—some *anybody* you met in the factory?"

I made a mistake. Wish I were living with Errol instead of trapping myself in her interrogation.

"I've never thought so irrationally. It can't be my genes."

Sorry I tried to love you. System tells us we grow up to live without you and Dad; I don't enjoy agreeing with the people who're trying to break me. If our last meeting had been the first, I would've kept the nicer idea of you.

"You're walking away? I'm not done—I'm not letting you tarnish your father's name by running off with a nobody!"

"He's a Class Seven," I shout from the door, a stone's throw from her bed. "I told you, but you were busy telling me he must be *ugly.*"

"Class Seven?" she cries, "You're climbing? Moira *Kennedy,* you are *not* climbing against the guidelines!"

"Right, that's for Nines." One foot inside.

"I can't believe you."

One foot outside. "I've got work tomorrow. Get a caretaker."

"Moira!"

Both steps leaving the apartment. The door slides shut behind me—hope she doesn't mind I left all identification with her. Where I'm driving, I'd rather not have it.

***

130

There, the story ends. Might as well quit. This isn't going where you want it to, and it won't. Inject me all you want. Go ahead. Stab it.

Too scared, huh? I have what you need somewhere, but your idiotic extraction ain't working, is it? Kill me already.

Ah, you can't. Convenient.

There's nothing else in the past to bribe me with, unless you wanna replay the day Errol and I agreed to—

Don't know what you're talking about.

Maybe these drugs are giving me brain cavities. Betcha didn't think of that one, pigshit.

Fine. I said go ahead, my arm's ready. It's a pincushion.

Yes, absolutely certain.

I'm—I don't care if—I've had worse, there's nothing there.

Nothing there. There's nothing.

***

No, no—I don't want this. I know what today is. Seti reminding me of her bond and how he's everything Hera intended; both our stations losing a few percent's worth from the rambling; it's Seti's fault I clock out a minute late, too, it really is. She hates me.

Clocked out? Behind, past a sunken shoulder, there's no line. The sorting room had emptied a while ago. Or was it seconds? I wasn't counting. I'll count in the following step.

Forward. No sound from the exit.

"Moira!"

Seti's heightened murmur hisses over the churning conveyor rhythm.

I shuffle back.

131

Oil drips from fingertips down to the palms, in between lifelines and scars. A trail in filthy, staining liquid, trickling across reddened wrists, falling from spasming forearms. My own.

He isn't here.

I think Seti's talking, again. Distracting—we have work to do. She's always shooting her mouth off at work. Company hasn't reprimanded her at all for the years I've been the listener, and she's been in sorting an additional year. It's her bond. Seti cowers under superstition, flinches around authority, and doesn't see how wrong it is for everything to be designed by them.

Metal pieces *thunk* onto others in their baskets. Left is bolts, right is…left is, right. Function by heart. Twenty-five years of memorization, data inputs through repetitive gesture and visual cues. Keep your head to the belt, then sweep the scrap metals into the baskets. When those are full, dump them into the chutes. Repeat.

Plodding footfalls hit the bleached concrete, rasping as the toecap etches along the ground. Stupid, ugly noise. It comes to a stop with a firm thud.

Fingers connected by wires, and plated in painted silver, hover above the conveyor belt. Where I'm working.

Monitor hands—why did they send in a robot?

Its moss-hued surface bears copper lines running from limb to limb; even as I hold my gaze at the passing items, the monitor's eye-bulbs shine through my head. Nobody forgets them once they've seen them. Sky blue if idle, watching, and no mistakes are detected; yellow if on alert; bright red—a stoplight's red—if it catches irregularity. I hunker down further.

Dropping a wire properly, the subtle clatter triggers a mental note. End of the week checks. That's the reason it's here.

I toss a bolt into the basket.

Errol's been missing for the sixth shift this week.

Screws are placed in the same one.

We aren't allowed communication outside of work, but people *have* built their own servers. I've found defectors' chatrooms at home.

Got a referral from someone without a name or face to remember them by. They're secure channels—the factory monitors won't discover anything.

But the police scouts are informed, and they notify the monitors.

I empty a somewhat overflowing basket, careful not to let the materials tip out. They rush into the chute, clumped together first, but with a jostle, they flow smooth as a faucet. Of rocks.

The monitor marches aside, inspecting Rob's section. I must be in the clear. Exhaling, the worry withdraws to the back of my mind. Yeah, these guys won't find me. The chatrooms are anonymous, just assigned names from a random set of words.

I wish Errol would sign up soon. He hadn't spoken against the idea, but he wasn't too excited about it. Unlike visiting him or talking groundhogs and machinery—face-to-face, he loves those topics.

"Y'alright, mate?"

"We're done?" I stutter, but keep working just in case.

Rob taps my arm, and I return a similar uncertainty. His mustache scrunches over some restrained frown.

"No, an hour left," he mutters. "Can you work faster?"

I don't owe you shit. "What?"

"You're slipping on them. Giving me more to sort, an' all."

"Yeah, sorry." I'm not sorry.

An hour is a long time—if I'm stopping by Errol's place, it'll be the minute I finish throwing scraps around. First foot out the door, sprint until the entrance. Maybe being late benefits me. I'll stay the night, instead—yeah. I will.

Hands are...dirty. Tar slops onto a frozen conveyor, path headlong to the factory floor; streaming through in opaque rivers; dripping from the belt parallel to mine.

A drooling goat stands atop the unmoving machine. Its horizontal pupils don't seem focused on much of anything. The blackened mess squeezes my arms as I look upon those yellow searchlights. The creature bleats, more glossy fluid pouring from its maw.

Curving, notched horns on its head are soaked in deeper black, but its fur is a yellowed white, not easily separated from the washed-out room. Silhouette broken only by red uniforms aligned behind its rotund figure. Scraggly fringes to the dangling hair. Pupils still fixated.

People tend to ignore things while time's ticking, but nobody would miss a goddamn goat in the middle of the room. They can't see it.

My arms work without needing vision, dexterity inherent by now. I'm sober. I've never ingested, injected, or snorted a single illicit substance. And I'm not a dumbass. Yelling and gesturing at a wild goat would drag me straight to counselling.

Have to leave soon.

The digital clock meanders onward, moments slowing to a crawl.

05-18-5004 11:09

Four-hour shifts shouldn't drag—they normally pass if I blink twice, not even three times. Tumbling parts linger on the belt. The oil trickles into my eyes. Squeezing them shut, tearing up, a stinging ache floods the blurring sight of a cluttered workspace. Unpolished silver and copper and aging steel muddle together as flecks rebound off them, from the ceiling lights, a glare like high beams at midnight.

Deprived of vision, I handle the sequence by touch. Weighing each article is second nature, though I'd be hard pressed to believe it's an inspiring feat. Obviously, things can be heavier than others. The screws have spirals, and their lengths are judged with minor difficulty—a freshmeat would pierce himself on the points, but I never will. With or without sight.

Wires—uncomplicated. We aren't required to untangle them, so tossing the coils aside is the only modicum of effort we suffer. It's not servicing a skyhog's transmission.

Smaller parts—nuts and washers—aren't the priority, but clearing them away into the screws' chute is basic practice. They'll slip from untrained or tired fingers, costing pay, meals, sometimes deserving write-ups. According to monitors, not us.

Can't miss a beat. I need the money—I've got plans.

The hum of the belt is undisturbed. Seti and Rob are awfully quiet—Seti, the most talkative drone I've met, is keeping silent.

It *has* to be nearly over.

I open an eye to clean palms. Above, same as always, it's the time:

05-18-5004 11:20

Forty left; it's two thirds to the end. Some goat is crying, and from where, from when, I'll never understand. There are no free-roaming animals in Limen-Hera. Least of all goats, the underutilized livestock. They don't let wild animals into factories, they don't let us leave of our own accord, they employ apathetic machines to police our shortcomings.

But that's how it's meant to be.

***

Wrong—you think I'm stupid? "How it's meant to be." Not in my vocabulary for this goddamned city of oxen, or whatever you're trying to raise.

Because of your system, I couldn't talk to Errol when he's sick, not without barging into his apartment. It doesn't bother you, though. You just replace him with someone else. I noticed. Maybe you think we're not paying attention, but everyone sees it.

What kind of question is that?

Yes, I stayed there with him. Didn't matter if I'd catch a cold, and I didn't. Three days passed before he returned to work; I was looking around, couldn't quite locate his funny hair, but somebody apparently moved him to another spot. Too far to walk beside him after our shift ended. Put him way over there. You did it on purpose.

135

Well, I don't care—you're the same. Hera's mutts.

He's here?

Don't lie. Stop lying.

Then bring him, show me. Or else you're lying.

Let me see him! Oh, there's nobody around with silver hair and eyes—then where is he? He's here, isn't he? If you took him away—

You better not have done this to him.

You're all filthy.

That's the arm—let go, get off, stop—please, please let—!

No, not counting!

Just let me see him, I'll tell you anything. I promise. All of it.

I will.

I will!

I'm...I'm gonna throw up.

***

Those untamed soon go rotten. Beaten down by the process, you fit into your place—any able-bodied worker's place—as a cell of Limen-Hera. You're both the fuel and the blood—you combust to make it move, serve its air to the lung of production. The city keeps us safe. The walls protect, the employers provide. All you have to do is give them your firstborn.

Secondborn, thirdborn, fourth—if the Class permits, you have the privilege of popping out another child. To prosper as Hera intended. Oh, unless the assignment tells otherwise. Forgot to mention. Didn't you know? If you're unwanted, your parents can set you to a lower Class. Yeah! I didn't either. Errol happened to have Threes for a mom and dad, but because they offered him up for experiments, he was dropped squarely in Class Seven.

Doesn't seem bad until I *really* think. At Ten, I can't go lower—well, I *can,* and I'll be on a watchlist. They might've shot down tracking chips for us, but the surveillance is widespread with the monitors in every workplace. Cops around the corner, ready to sic those bots on us so they don't have to fight.

This isn't about them. It's about me and Errol and the obvious pitfalls of us contributing to Limen-Hera. Against the law. Now that I've slept on it, begging Errol to reset his bond is the stupidest thing I've ever considered. I'll be relying on luck. Population over a million, around eighty percent at Class Seven and below, sixty from Classes Eight through Twelve. Chances are he'll draw three women—none of them me.

I don't even want kids. This hellhole doesn't deserve to abuse a child from him. And what if Errol's genetics are faulty? Perhaps the hair and eye color modifications come with hidden mutations, or they'll cause birth defects—perhaps, scientifically, the innovators haven't tested the procedure enough to predict what it'll do. It's not like they publish their reports, anyway. Nobody can choose to be born somewhere else; if I could send my kid off on the railway to freedom, I would smuggle the next generation across city borders.

What a farce—I can't do shit, I'm sleeping on cardboard. A year's gone. No apocalypse came to whisk me away.

The grimy, permanent stench from rain-soaked tents leaks into my bod— garbage bag, I mean, blanket. Haven't touched clean cotton for a while, though I'll make arrangements to. Simply forgot I'm an emotional wreck fixing wrecked cars for a living. How silly of me!

I shut my mouth before it lazily falls open. Didn't actually sleep, just laid here, thinking, plotting, tasting bile. Either I'm breathing tainted air, or swallowing my own stomach. The soup wouldn't agree with me. After smelling the stewpot these bastards cooked up, I fed the charity's meal to the ground like a bird to her little hatchlings. Apparently, pavement didn't accept recycled food, and neither did the rebel commune.

So, they had my tent arrogated to the unshaven man who wandered in yesterday. My bag of scrap metal was in there. He spontaneously vacated the premises—with *my* scrap metal. Now, I am broke.

I would've liquidated my remaining assets, but then I'd be running around naked. I've seen guys sell the shirts off their back. Muddy coveralls are a two-in-one deal I'm not willing to auction. I bet used underwear would put me back in the black, if I didn't mind the skeeviest, most degenerate bidders prying it from me. Basically, if I had no dignity. Can't lose the last of it just yet.

Hope is in the paper. They—the upstarts—print their own currency with the help of a mole in Class Seven. Word on the telephone line claims this underground economy had been around for...a time, casting money and coinage into the market once more. These de facto dollars don't get you a single donut from a self-serve bakery, but they do exchange well if you're in the mood for dried fish and a sack of rice. Suddenly, when life plunges to Class Eleven, businesses with giant *NO CASH* signs become more than discouraging. As much as *VIOLATORS WILL BE REPORTED.*

Wouldn't dare to let go of this wallet, even if sidewalk patrol tries to wrench it from my hands. Pretending to hug myself, I hold in what little heat the evening allows. Twenty dollars is a start. Measly compared to the credit system, except untraceable. Repair a few more rust buckets and dying groundhogs, then I'll earn myself new stolen clothes, and a good meal.

It's been so long, I never realized the shit-smell and piss-stains reek more than bleach. At least the latter kills you.

What dumb bitch would believe in a resistance having some secret hideout? Who else? God, I hate it. This is the first commune to lack pipe-wielding meatheads, and it's no improvement. In fact, I miss the raving doomsayer from the last group, the spot several streets north. South? I know I ran through some alleyways.

Hera was merciful in letting me lose the monitor I'd provoked; not directly, but after bashing a skinny junkie's skull in, I had to bolt. Maybe whoever stole my goods yesterday did me a favor. The self-defense weapon may have fingerprints on it—wait a minute. Prints. Wonder if Mom kept my ID? She better have tossed it. No, city records exist, too. Damn, I should hurry. Plan E won't work by itself.

"Cold...kinda warm...I need to..."

Someone grumbling from the side, rustling within his tent. Sounds like the guy with the eyebrow-mole. My chosen neighbor, since he's harmless until proven hostile. Not speaking of his hygiene.

This defecator—*defector* leaves his unzipped home, wrestling the broken zipper he can't and won't replace. Man needs something to be angry at, I guess. Upon telling off the door, he stumbles to his feet, taking a trip down the road.

Thinking about it, I'd enjoy a shower tonight. Implicitly, it's optional to everyone in this community. Call me a double dissident, but I support cleanliness, especially baths. Although, it's a chore to harvest from public bathrooms; danger lurks wherever the cameras point. Bottles are hard to come by, too. I'm thankful I plucked the cleanest one from a trashcan. It's a fresh bottle, uncrumpled plastic, small enough for stuffing into my coveralls. But it doesn't carry much.

Just a rinse before I leave, then. Kicking off the garbage blanket, I push up with the good arm. Twisted the dominant wrist when I'd whacked that other guy—aches if I bend it a certain way, but it's nothing a daily stretch can't help. When everything's a dull pain, the body grows numb.

Most people use streetlights as checkpoints in the dead of night. I've lived past my Class Eleven anniversary, which is lovely, because I've learned to follow the shadows instead. This city has various LED guides to accent the walls and roads, as dim as they are. Further from Limen-Hera's center, infrastructure takes a backseat to herding the homeless to and fro. Class Sevens are busier tending to the power grid. They neglect damaged wires outside of buildings—explains the flickering streetlamps.

Someone high off her mind had bumped into a streetlamp, once. Saw a monitor seize her arms like its hands were makeshift cuffs. I'd waited. You don't get to witness this every day, after all. But the police didn't arrive, and I wasn't about to stand and watch while a shrieking bitch flailed around. This was before the bashing incident— before monitors would have a reason to recognize me. Let's just say I've scratched "being vice-gripped by a monitor bot" from the bucket list.

An uncanny splotch shifts on the corner. Across the street. Again, it rushes under a trembling light. The lump of a water bottle sits comfortably at my waist, lukewarm. I continue. Weaving into darkness, eyes hooked on the other side. Slide the bottle upward, gently, don't crinkle it. Pop it out from the collar. I'll bathe another time—kind of thirsty.

Screw off the cap, set it to my lips. I pass the busted light, walking parallel, studying where the silhouette had been.

Almost forgot I'm holding my wallet.

Surrounding apartments have their windows shut, the scarce room or two bright enough to navigate by. Pausing at the intersection, I slip both belongings into a pocket, hand resting over, protecting them. From nobody, right now. It could be somebody if I don't leave.

I look up. Not plain to see, I assume this sign marks Court and Bancway. Farther south than I'd thought.

"Wehh…"

There—was that a—?

It bleats somewhat higher, nothing toward the Court. But down on Bancway, trotting along the rightmost sidewalk, is a goat. Not nothing.

I wave. I don't think it's unreasonable to wave. It can't return the gesture, but it nags at me in kind.

"Mehhh!"

Don't—don't run off! I dash across the street after a goat. A *goat*. It was only an impulse, to follow, but as it jumps ahead, I salivate. Spent months starving. Humanity's worst hasn't sunken to cannibalism—a miracle—despite the scarcity of meat. Don't get me wrong, they have to exist. I've probably never met a cannibal because Hera knows I'll give up. I'm smaller, lower on the food chain. If there were pigeons, someone's already roasted them into extinction, which leaves—

The goat squeaks and playfully skips onward.

I'm bigger. I can catch it.

"Weh-eh!"

How do you prepare goats? Can you cook 'em? Do they taste okay? Whatever, I'll find out.

City streets blend into each other if you don't pay attention. Darting in the tailwind of a speeding goat, I bound an extra inch, then a foot, and pump all energy into my legs. I'm gaining a hair. But the goat noisily protests, outpacing me against the odds. I swipe and miss its tail.

"Sonuvabitch." I cough. "Get. Back. *Here.*"

My foot sticks in a sludge, taking all of me down with it. Splattering against pitch-black ground. I shove myself upward, spitting tar onto the roadside; plies of gunk split from my uniform; but in struggling out, I only sink.

Human screams—I chance a look above, the goat's nose meeting mine.

The beast yells again, blackened throat teeming with holes, its teeth uncannily normal. I start laughing. It's just a goat, and I can't catch it, not at all. There's a tarpit in the middle of the city. Who thought it was a good idea to build things here? Be careful, somebody might trip! Great, it's great!

Bleeding scrapes run from my elbows to the back of each hand—I ate it, alright. I guess it's supposed to burn. Funny, seeing as the chilled breeze doesn't hurt. Stupid goat.

"Hey," I tell the creature, "hey, you think—*haha*—think you could, maybe, call an ambulance?"

Its yellow stare doesn't move.

"Hey. I'm gonna die."

Not a sound.

"I'm hungry, please, I just want—"

***

Shocks rupture at pointed electrodes—neck, wrists, arms, chest. Heart thumps. The stale room reeks of burnt hair and formaldehyde, making every inhale a pain of its own. Tremors plague every limb, though they're rigid, barely twitching. I can't make a fist.

Grids mark the concrete floor. What must be a few steps across, there's another wooden chair, identical to this—leg restraints, belts for the arms, too. Wires and round patches. The crown headrest.

Electricity shoots through again, stronger. Everything seizes up. I force my head down, locking my chin there—no, can't breathe like this—I lift it slightly, watching the other seat.

I suck air between chattering teeth.

"Keep your eyes down." An order from the interrogation officer.

Her glossy boots are followed by a second pair—rough leather, thick cloth dimpled at where the edges meet. They're beige working clothes.

"Did I not make myself clear?" she says.

I obey, a recurrent pain reminding me why I should.

"You have a visitor." She steps beside the matching chair, leading that oddly familiar uniform over. "I don't think you'll need any introductions."

Freezing sweat trickles from my face.

Circling around, she doesn't speak, a loud *click* accompanying the metal clasps closing at the visitor's calves. It can't be anyone but him. I wish it weren't; he shouldn't be involved.

The officer strides between us, not before adding, "Once you both agree to our terms, then you're free to leave. Until then, please, do talk. We won't stop you."

She promptly marches outside. Numerous locks tick at the door. She'll be listening, her and the cop who tackled me. I can guess what they're anticipating I'll say, but there's an issue: I forgot where the commune was. I don't know the leaders of those defect groups. Can't be sure they had leaders at all—they're all nutcases. Hyped on adrenaline, drunk off chemical-flavored liquor, sick in the stomach and the brain. I'm not with them. I want out, but I'm not going along with them.

"So, is this where you went?"

And now I've roped him into this.

"Must've snapped your legs back there." Errol shifts his knees, but the restraints keep them from moving much. "How'd you land and take off running?"

I can't believe they caught him so fast. "Wanted out."

He taps his boots to an alternating tempo.

"Had some energy left, said 'fuck it,' and jumped," I endeavor. A spasm pulses through a jugular.

He chuckles—at a time like this. "You're crazier than I thought. Glad I live in Room One-o-two…or *lived,* if they're planning on relocating me. No way they wouldn't. What're they putting on the record?"

Take a guess.

" 'Designation something-something, found guilty of staring longingly into an unapproved woman's eyes.' Put the monster in solitary!"

Fine, I'll laugh. But I won't enjoy it.

"Conveniently forgot you kissed me," I remark.

"Oh, I didn't, isn't possible. Fuckin' weird. Felt like a pair of bricks pushing together—"

The joy fizzles too soon. "Yeah."

"—didn't it?"

"Yeah, it did."

We both pretend we hadn't mocked the event, letting the hollow quiet have the floor. Acid—or whatever they'd jabbed into me—won't blot out my memory, either. Errol said I'd wanted it to happen. It's true, it really is, but he'd explained back my reasoning as if he'd been holding an intervention. Asking if I was happy. I think I'd nodded, and then he leaned over; we became bond-breakers for the most awkward display in history. Was I content? I'd met the goal, he said. We'd exchanged the first obligatory affection, like some immature novel. Errol stated he'd agree to love if I had a plan. He meant it.

It'd gone over perfectly, so I ran.

"Well, you were right about the drugs," I say, "not from before the past, but after then. Now."

Errol stops fidgeting. Doesn't reiterate who I am today or even sound like he's breathing, if that's possible.

I raise a glance to his silver eyes—sparks roll under my skin. They amplify— triggering the shakes again. A beat—a yell—two shouted profanities.

"Shit," Errol hisses. "What millennium is it? Didn't they ban the chair?"

Is he alright? We lock eyes—the same shockwave strikes.

"They—" I bite my lip when the next tremor kicks. I'd start crying if I wasn't completely exhausted. They're not only targeting me for their benefit; they're harming him.

Errol hiccups, labored breaths cutting the deadened room.

Lying pricks. Let me see him, and I talk. Those were the terms, simple, you couldn't have made any mistakes. "Filthy bas—"

Every fight to catch his eyes sparks off the chairs, intensity fluctuating with each surge; sometimes a dull blow from a wrench; or hundreds of screwdrivers, piercing down to the bone; as nasty as the aftershocks that follow, their fainter vibrations tormenting the brain— my very soul—more than a convulsing body. I just want to look—

"Head down!" Errol interjects.

I tremble, though the electricity is already dissipating. My body won't bend. "I can't."

"Then don't look!"

I shut my eyes, screaming at him, "I'm not!"

He and I unwittingly stare for a split second. Am I getting used to it? Our chairs smite us, but the bursts tread almost delicately. I can't tell. Pinching, or abrupt chain lightning. Hurts regardless. I keep both eyelids sealed.

"Stay still," Errol murmurs.

All I offer is blocked vision and involuntary shivers. Surviving the singed hair proves just as nauseating, its sharp odor unmistakable. Blood dries on my flaking lips. I bit the spot again.

Errol groans like he's as fed up as I am.

"It happens when you—" His fingernails scratch the splintering armrests. "Happens...when we look at each other."

The realization falls from him, descending a step at a time, his tone flattening by its last word.

"Of course, it does," he says, sighing.

"Because they're watching."

I take his silence as agreement. He'd tell me if he thought otherwise; he normally would.

They can't kill us yet: we have value. Information, for example, on the whereabouts of alleged terrorists. Don't think they'll need an answer, even if I had one; the communes do a fine job of quashing their own rebellions. Errol is reduced to an incentive—like I'd sell out for him. Too much effort for a confession too late.

Weird that they're punishing him if I'm the sole defector he's collaborated with, and his worst crime is bond-breaking. Meanwhile, I have theft; operating an unlicensed business to sell on government property; general trespassing; public indecency; violating the employment contract; more theft; all sorts of guilt by association;—and didn't they accuse me of drug usage? Or was it the sale? I've done neither of those, but they're convinced I'm an addict. I can't even get addicted to love. God, have to keep words to myself—what a dumbass statement. Love isn't something you snort, anyway.

"Huh. A shock whenever we look at each other," I end up saying. "I didn't know it was a felony. Maybe a minor offense, I'll give 'em that, but the chair's excessive force."

"Maybe," Errol adds.

Absolutely, not maybe.

Another thing's nagging me. Not a hum to indicate the location of their power source, so I guess, if a generator exists, it must be in a different room. There's more to this nowhere place. Prison or correctional, or both. Our curriculums don't prepare us for incarceration—concerning prisons, they're as transparent as Limen walls. Bashing your head through isn't going to work. Struggle to climb it, peek over the top, and you're asking to fall, dying whether it's forward or backward. Choose to tunnel underneath, someone buries the hole you made.

"Only path outside is..." I tilt my head, stealing a glimpse of the door. "A gateway."

Errol's leg twitches. "And if they don't let you through?"

"Keep trying."

"No matter what?"

"Faith depends on you."

He doesn't respond—doesn't laugh, sigh, grumble.

We're isolated. Cops aren't going to open the exit unless they've had their fill. No more bending, no breaking; as long as we're here, I'll endure ignoring him. It won't be forever. Without a clock, the numbered minutes and hours aren't real, just pretend. They'll have my answer on my terms, since they botched the compromise. None of the satisfaction for 'em. I can't and won't picture Errol with a furrowed brow. Don't need to see him defeated.

I'd rather remember him smiling.

***

Pins scuttle along my calves, static prancing across goosebumps, playing hopscotch on an empty lot. If I don't stretch each finger or wriggle the toes, all presence rises to a floating head. Haven't opened my eyes, but I refuse to sleep. Lost count of the pulse. Fifteen seconds—I've been estimating by the heartbeat possessing an ear, opposite side ringing constantly. Feigned peace doesn't fool my brain anymore.

We haven't spoken beyond twenty minutes—I couldn't keep ticking them, no motivation—while our singular escape route holds

146

shut. Officers don't come in. Errol intermittently flicks his armrest, jogs both knees, repositions his boots, and the order always changes. At first, I'd observed the common motions with a straightened gaze. 'Til every sound had a visual, and I grew bored, I'd thought—no, it's paranoia. A slight look would set off the electricity, I knew. That's the reason I closed them for good.

Errol's getting colder. If I am, he is. Our stomachs gave up grumbling; I lick the sourness sticking around my teeth as if it'll satisfy, but the idea of food twists a knot inside. Plaiting the intestines, maybe. Anatomy diagrams imply they're lengthy enough to braid. Once we're freed—when they realize I'm as stupid as I talk—I'm taking Errol to lunch. A final meal before accepting our differences. The usual fried, processed food.

Those sodium levels inspire a craving, spilling into thirst. Drool wells up to my tongue—I swallow. The sound of a single gulp is deafening to heightened hearing. In fact more senses seem to work too well for me. Errol's twiddling around isn't restricted to his lower half— I'm positive, really.

Sometimes, when the seated part calms, I swear the vibrations imply shrugging shoulders, or rolling a crick out of his neck. It isn't as obvious as, say, the moments he sniffs a bit too forcefully. But I'm sure he's shifting on purpose, for circulation. Meanwhile, I don't want to provoke anything. There's the soreness in my dominant arm coupled with phantom shocks, which aren't very discriminating. Going numb is painless. Unless I move again.

"Hey."

Errol's voice passes for another jolt.

"What?" I'm not concerned if I sound harsh.

"Can you just tell them?"

"No."

"Why not?" He's also turned bitter, the way his accusation snaps.

"Because I have no idea." Might as well admit it—if they'll finally open the door. "The 'terrorists' are everywhere. In small groups, no secret underground base, and where I was, no real weapons. A few shivs, but"—I avert from Errol's face, addressing the security camera with wide eyes—"listen, they're just a bunch of lost, hopeless men. Disillusioned people stagnating close to the sewers. I don't know how many streets I'd lived on, if they were the northern or nearing the center."

Can they hear me?

"I was wrong. It's hell," I speak up. "At least let Errol go, he had nothing to do with—!"

He scoffs.

I look at him—shit, wait—I find the wall and brace for it. The pain's late. Actually, it doesn't spark, not once. We saw each other, didn't we? His hair and eyes haven't changed—hasn't been a century, so I can't understand the conclusion I've jumped to. As if he'd age in a day. And I'm right—he doesn't frown. It wasn't a smile but he wasn't pissed off. I'm glad. Spit straggles on my chin, dripping to the ground— I should've downed the saliva. Well, no harm no foul, I hadn't noticed. Still waiting on the shocks. Didn't we...?

"My God," Errol says, forcing an exhale, "phew, you scared me, damn—terrorist, what the—you thought it was about *that?*"

"What else! I'm just trying to end this, alright? It has to be that, it's not the bond-breaking!"

"It *is.*"

You're kidding.

"Officer Seven-One, I think, some number with a seven. She said I'm here until you plead guilty on breaking your bond."

I fixate on the wall—don't glare at him.

"Believe me, I don't think it's any less stupid. I didn't even—"

"Fuck you."

Silver encapsulates his pupils, the partial smirk slipping. The electrodes tingle. Hardly a real sensation.

"I'm not crazy, I know they wanted me to rat the commune out or something, or give them an address, anything." I jerk the restraints, rattling the belt buckles. "You should've said something, asshole!"

"I could've, but I—"

"It would have been *so* much easier if you told me, Errol!" My chair creaks. "Save us from being stuck in a torture chamber, yeah? The hunger, the burns? Everything?"

He leans back, appearing more comfortable than he should.

"You admit it, then?" he asks.

"Yes! I sat there and did nothing—because I didn't think you'd kiss me, or whatever you did, but you did. I did!" None of the phrases formulate before jumbling up, and the only thing pouring out is an irrepressible, slobbering nonsense. I'm hungrier, thirstier now—hours wasted on him. Bond-breaking? Must mean theft is borrowing something, then immediately putting it down. That's what we did. And it wasn't enough, it was the second worst disappointment I'd suffered. The first being my idiotic, cowardly decision to jump out the nearest window, instead of pulling him in by the shirt—

Disgusting. I can't wipe my face.

Both officers rush into the room, two greener-clad soldiers shoving past to seize my arms. The belts had come loose. The door had unlocked. Trivial compared to dealing with the smiling douchebag ahead—I wobble into the additional hands.

"Stand down!" the left one commands.

The right soldier could dislocate that shoulder he's digging his fingers into, the bastard.

Officer Seven-Something kneels her body close, and I glance below. My legs were still confined to the chair's. She unfastens the clasps, setting them loose. After sitting through pain, wholly immobilized, I can't stand. Frankly, I don't believe I've ever had legs. Reality prefers to lie, anyhow.

The soldiers yank me upright.

"Take her for further questioning," says the other officer—a fatass, as most of them are. He liberates Errol from the chair. "You, you're free to go. Come on."

I'm dragged behind Errol and his escort, my ankles sliding along the floor.

"Wait!" I exclaim, throat rasping. "I'm talking to him!"

We're taken into a narrow corridor, the soldiers supporting me against the wall. Errol halts between the doors across, looking down on my sunken posture. The fat man hasn't loosened his grip.

"Make it quick, Kennedy," the officer threatens.

His partner puts her hands on her hips.

"Errol." Met with a solemn face, I hesitate. Even if the question's lingering on my tongue.

"Yeah?" Curt and uninterested.

"Why didn't you tell me?"

He also pauses, ogling the hand squeezing his arm. I try to steady these useless legs.

"We didn't do anything wrong," he expresses in a lowered, soothing breath. "I was afraid you'd…if being illegal would make you leave, and…"

Salivating again. I can't understand him looking this intently, not at some ugly, twitching expression.

"Made me sick to call it a crime. It just felt right."

I laugh for a second. Our respective escorts guide us in opposing directions, hauling my unbalanced form while he gets to walk away, unimpeded. Yes, I think the officer let go. I search over a shoulder, then the other—they're making conversation? Errol is showing his back. He's not going to turn around?

A rough cloth scrubs my grin off. Seven-Something is grimacing, pinching the handkerchief as if she's carrying all the world's disease.

"God's sake, Kennedy," she grumbles.

I ingest a mouthful of spit, licking dry lips. He meant it; I believe in him. One final, longing glance behind. My neck twinges.

A blink captures it. Yellow blots shining from the corridor—now an unending void—and a streak of oil across the floor. Moisture gathers at my feet. Black stains on the tattered pants, grease coating everything past both ankles.

I shouldn't be thrilled to have seen him. He didn't smile back.

***

Spark plugs clatter onto the workbench, a stray rolling off and rattling against concrete. Crouching, I take a blind swipe for it, tossing the piece with its other used cohorts. Once I straighten up, the littered bench calls to instinct. *Clean me!* It's such a mess. Unfortunately, moving parts and tools would result in them getting misplaced. I'll resist the urge to shove everything off. The clutter has harmony obscured by its chaos—I'm supposed to memorize wherever I find things. Not paid to organize anymore.

From my right, some wrench is thrown in a pile.

An emptied box nudges me.

"Here, pile them in."

I wipe my mouth, focusing on his hand. The plugs fill the temporary disposal, a bit too high, but it'll do. Shove them aside for the time being.

"Checked the hover-disks?" I ask.

"Triple-checked."

"Filters?"

He shakes his head, amused. "Think I missed one."

I hold a breath. Errol's arm bumps me quite blatantly, though he doesn't apologize or acknowledge himself.

Hands, hands. This grime won't rub clean—I wipe each palm over the uniform's sleeves, ignoring the thought of his coarse fingertips. *I hate him.* That's true, I did decide to despise him. Since the...negotiation. From then on, the reassignment's blessing had been the cruelest curse. They're rewarding me for staying quiet. They've purged the streets, I heard. The commute home is evidence enough,

151

eerily barren where the dodgiest vagrants used to roam. As if they'd never dirtied the sidewalks from the start.

All for the best of Hera.

It'll be normal, again. I'm in the career I'd yearned for with the man I—no, I have to hate him. Stop grinning like an idiot.

"Moira? Could you find me an air filter?" Errol stoops over the skyhog's gaping hood, looking here expectantly.

"Just a sec, Errol!" I shuffle the various boxes around. There. Exactly the thing, smack dab next to the other filters. *Of course.*

"Moira!"

The goat halts its prance around my legs.

"Sorry, yes?" Carrying the filter, I swivel on a heel.

A man with tied-back, auburn hair gawks from the car.

"Is that a nickname or something?" he asks. "Don't know how, exactly, but if you say so…"

I hurry to the man's side, thrusting the box into his offered hand.

"No, sorry, I was distracted," I answer, "don't worry about it."

He gives a halfhearted shrug. "Sure, no big deal."

For him, maybe. Axel doesn't take anything seriously enough. He could've asked if I was feeling okay, and yet he didn't. I remember someone who would've.

Although I dart back to the workbench, alone, the moment I reach it, Axel's hands arrive to pinch my waist. A familiar current prickles from the touch. My assigned bond holds me from behind, chuckling. Oh, comfortable, are we?

"We're working." I find the new spark plug.

"Aw, I *also* love you," Axel croons, snuggling close; but his voice soon rumbles lower. "Wouldn't hurt to lighten up."

When an elbow greets his rib, he whines—I didn't knock him that hard. He mumbles while pacing back to the open hood, nursing the blow to his midsection with a few thoughtful pats. The complaints under his breath aren't worth a credit. I never wanted a stranger here.

Delicate hoofprints spread the day's work about my untidy bench; I watch the goat resume frolicking, his bleating quieter than usual. He should be miserable. I crumple the box around the plug, fist balling as tight as it'll go. And throw it at the goat's head.

Clink. Oops, I hit the floor instead. Stupid.

"The hell are you doing, Moira?" Axel yells, setting down a wrench.

I turn around. Try to smile at him.

"Killing an annoying bug."

"You wreck it, we'll both pay for it." He sighs as he's walking around the vehicle, a pensive stare aimed into its guts. "How'd a bug get in?"

"Dunno, maybe it's because the garage is wide open."

Axel puffs. A stray hair flies up, then lands right where it'd been.

"Sorry, it was a huge...bug." I couldn't find a specific excuse. Bugs aren't uncommon, though I was too tongue-tied upholding the front. *Cockroach* would've sufficed. Dammit.

Really, it's the worst lie I've ever told, but he wouldn't have believed me if I'd said it was a snake. I sure as hell won't kill the goat, either. In spite of the reflexive pain at the thought of him, his eyes bringing nothing more than torment, I'll take him to heart; and although the once distinct features blend into masculine genericism, they may be the last I'll see if I put the brakes on reality and imagine a different future. But I guess I'm not the future—I've been idling in the present since birth. Accounting for time is useless. It'll tick away while the world refuses to stop, our cities running on their beastly engines.

Ignoring all adversity in mind, an onerous goat trots beside me on knobby legs. Its teeth start to gnaw at my ankle. Yes, I've had the good and the bad. I'm no arbiter of life. I'd be a fool to fight with the closest thing I've felt to love. How could I ever lead it to the slaughter?

Cornered: Open Grave

I've always wondered what the Earth's core looked like, down in those supposed molten innards around her rocky heart. Each morning, ever since I could walk, I had crawled between a gash in the fence, earning a scar on my back, skinning my hands and knees; I sought out an odd calling. Down the pavement broken by roots and over my neighbor's lawn. Across the road after looking both ways, as my mother instilled. Where brick-laid housing had parted, there was that man-made forest beyond a chain-link fence.

"Come help us," it said—I never quite saw what *it* was. Some visits it had sounded close to a woman like Aunt Theresa, vocal cords retching and hoarse with emphysema. Weak, feeble noises I followed because I wasn't a coward. If it hadn't reminded me of her, I would've played inside.

But I did wander. The route seemed invisible to any eyes except mine, as if I'd been born a compass fixed to its direction. I couldn't stray without hearing its voice. Other children—those who'd acquired a sense of strangers—wouldn't have pursued her. Dreams of walking there with my aunt had altered reality, then. I reasoned she'd been waiting there, and if I'd gone alone, we'd sneak to the playground together. My mother wouldn't have allowed it.

I never knew if there was a playground in the park. My imagination believed it, so I did too. A single swing set and jungle gym were everything, and best of all, it was a secret place. Though I wasn't allowed to watch many movies about them, I had an affinity for fairytales. Fairies, really. Elves, gnomes, sprites of nature. That there was something smaller than myself only I could perceive—because I wasn't an adult—made me all the more excited to run off on my own.

I'd take the path I memorized, but each time, an officer would help me home if I went too far. His patrol didn't deter my ambitions; I ran through the entrance again and again, escorted out again and again; I eventually knew the man by name, though I've since forgotten. I think it started with a G.

"Sorry, kid," he'd say to a pouting boy. "Can't have you gettin' lost or hurt 'round here."

"Wanna go play." I was about four or five, and not the brightest—I'm lucky I can picture it. Me and my dirtied overalls and lopsided suspenders, toddling on sneakers with loose laces.

"You can play somewhere else." Officer G said this nicely. More carefully than I'd have expected from adults at the time.

"Wanna go play—with Auntie!"

"Your Auntie? She ain't here. C'mon, le's get you home."

"Noooo!"

I would whine and cry, but take his hand anyway. It worried my parents sick, they claimed; they never thought to stop me the next morning.

The long-awaited time had come when I'd infiltrated the depths of those trees and bushes. Officer G was nowhere in sight. No birds or squirrels. Not a sound prevailing over rustling foliage. Sunlight poked through this itchy hiding place, with a gentle brush against my chubby face.

"Come here, help us."

I fumbled out of the leaves. While the hiss repeated, I yelled for Aunt Theresa, but she didn't say anything else.

Then:

"Come here, Arthur."

Although I returned to the gravelly pathway, I wasn't any less confused, or lost. Or frightened. And so the compass would still point to her—I couldn't trust myself to go back. Besides, it would've been a waste to journey this far, only to risk Officer G catching me like he'd done before. I was a boy on a mission. I'd find Auntie even if it took the scariest road to get there.

Roads can be tedious, but they're not boundless.

I stopped near the end. Bits of pavement were shattered at the clearing, dirt packed over its pieces, weeds sprouting up as grass choked underneath. Clovers hid in patches, but the wiry, leafless bushes aired themselves in plain view. The trees here had lost their leaves, too—it was the middle of spring.

Marveling at absolutely everything, I sat down to rest my short, tired legs. I gawked above several times. Clouds hadn't blotted all the sky's blues, but they were puffed up with rain. Close to raining, but not quite. Maybe I'd only imagined the droplet hitting my nose. Then, my right arm.

"Come help us, please."

It spoke clearer from a particular space; I found her ahead of the path, though she wasn't there. White mushrooms ran a ring around Auntie's cries. Louder still, it chanted until I crouched in the circle, staring through its middle.

"Are you stuck, Auntie?" I said at a displaced thumbprint of soil.

"Yes, yes. Help us."

I poked a finger into the dry dirt to start digging her out, but it wasn't working. Trying another finger, I drove it into the earth, twisting and scratching as particles flicked aside, revealing more of the same. Noon had beaten my shoulders with the sun's rays. I dug as far as I could, though eventually, I would inevitably grow hungry and sleepy.

"Mommy will be sad if I don't go back," I would explain to the ground, patting it affirmatively. "Wait here, Auntie. I'll come back tomorrow."

She said nothing in return; it breathed roughly, gasping for air.

The child I was had strangely accepted uncanny requests from the ground itself. Backpedaling across the crumbled pavement, nearly tripping, wasting precious seconds, kicking up the dense weeds, to straggle off the beaten path and find home. Countless repetitions of the route had drawn a map within my head, though I would've had trouble putting it to paper. Along with the compass, so too would the map remain in thought.

As promised, I had bolted for the park first thing in the morning, and Auntie still spoke from that circle. It didn't occur to me a person couldn't breathe underground. I'd figured if there was a core to the Earth, then it was hollow. Aunt Theresa didn't have the strength for most things; she couldn't possibly climb up herself, not without my help. She said so.

The hole would grow in size by an uneven margin, clawed through as if an animal decided to burrow in, some creature no bigger than a worm. I wouldn't tell anyone—I had the instinct not to. Boys my age enforced a normalcy in the classroom, by word and fist—sometimes teeth—which obviously shunned those with unusual hobbies. Saving Aunt Theresa was no hobby to me, of course, but I couldn't admit that. I had some common sense.

School had soon taken the dawning hours from me, but I wasn't allowed to run off in the evening. I was *five*. Even my mother wouldn't have exceptions for this—our doors were locked, and the front door in particular had a squeal to wake the neighbors upstairs and downstairs, even adjacent to us.

I remember unlatching the window and pushing it above my head. Humid air hung over the confined townhouses, the wind absent, streetlights guiding me onto the sidewalk. I'd halted at the first in a sanctuary of glowing safety. What if I really did get lost?

"Help, help us. Please."

And joining the voice was always the compass, pointing to her.

The task became an obligation. Auntie was down there, crying, begging *me* to pull her out of the soil. I had to help. Rainstorms would flood the park during the summer, and I'd run home covered in mud. I had to keep going. Loosened earth would work against my efforts to tunnel deeper; I'd kick the puddle away, sending a slurry of brownish grime from the hole. It stopped raining weeks later, so I'd put the biggest rocks I could find to keep the ground from settling into itself. Auntie still wept somewhere below.

For uncountable days, I scraped away with dirtied fingernails.

My parents never had the money for things. As a teen, I no longer had an aunt to spoil me with ice cream and action figures and whatever construction kit I'd only given a glance. She'd spent money as easily as my mother and father, but spent it on the right things. Things not right for herself, but things her loved ones coveted. I cherished them less than her. She'd married quite rich—her charity had been my uncle's wealth, which, to this day, hasn't run dry, though he hadn't visited once her lungs had given out. Without Auntie, I didn't want much anymore. I couldn't want. There was no one to give.

Without a thought, I followed my heart, visiting the circle again. Someone had filled the hole. Whoever it was, they didn't damage the ring around it, but packed in dirt as if to fortify a road. It wouldn't budge. Maybe my hands and strength had improved after eight years, I assumed—wrongly. No scrabbling or yelling could pull the earth apart. Throwing pebbles aside, I looked into the measly damage I'd inflicted. A pinhole. Nothing.

A sharper stone caught my eye. Better than *nothing.* Though it rubbed my palm raw, I stabbed at the spot and—it made me smile—the haphazard marks gave way to the hole once more. Those smoother stones I'd left were still buried there. They dislodged without more than a shimmy and a twist, lighter than I'd felt them before.

While tossing the rocks behind, I stopped suddenly, listening to a breeze swishing through the clearing. The voice hadn't spoken in a while.

"Are you there?" I said.

At thirteen, I didn't believe in Santa Claus, and yet I had some inkling the circle could still talk to me. After all, no one could prove otherwise.

"Auntie?" I whispered, chucking a rock forward.

Lifting a handful, I dropped them in a messy pile, just outside the circle. Silly of me to have thought she'd answer. Once the remaining stones were removed, the earth became too solid for the crude tool I'd equipped; the pointed rock was now blunt and chipped in places. I discarded it like the others.

Not saying another word to her.

One day, I got a new idea. I took a few classmates into the park. Barrel (also called Fat Barry) and Tristan. I'd required a shovel and a spade or two, implements Tristan agreed to lend if my fibbing miraculously turned out true. Barry was easy; he didn't question. Honestly, how'd I ever persuade Tristan? The trick stunk. I hadn't said a thing of the rumored voice, but—as ridiculous as it might sound—I'd lied about buried treasure. They were older, probably smarter than me. Except I assumed those months they had on me didn't mean much. After all, if the story worked, they had to be dumb. Logic isn't my sharpest tool.

Whether they'd believed me or not, I led them to the clearing. They judged the circle for themselves.

"This sucks," said Barrel.

Tristan broke out into the worst fit of laughter, bowling over himself. He only managed to point and gasp.

"I'm not joking!" I shouted, heading closer to the hole. "Why would there be a circle and no treasure?"

"He actually dug a freakin' *hole.*" Tristan wheezed.

So, that's it. They went along with skipping school to make fun of me.

I picked up a rock.

"Maybe he's looking for earthworms. Jacob loves those." Barrel tapped Tristan's arm.

"Yeah!" Tristan wheezed again after his last laugh. Cupping his hands, he yelled through them, "Hey, hey! Look at me! You hungry? Gonna eat some *worms?*"

There was no forethought—when they'd faced each other again, I threw the rock at Tristan.

A jagged slice ran across his cheek. He touched it, saw the blood, then me, and glared like I'd provoked a feral cat.

Fat Barry was already barreling toward me faster than Tristan. Heavier than him, too. If I couldn't dig with my bare hands, stopping Barrel with them was a senseless idea. Instead of running, I hunkered down, grabbing him the way those wrestlers on TV did. We were fighting in a ring of our own, but I hadn't considered two things: I would've been far below Barrel's weight class, and everything my father watched was fake. Thirteen-year-old me didn't know. Didn't have the seconds needed to calculate an attack. I couldn't lift that fatass—I can't believe I tried.

Barrel tackled me to the dirt and dying grass. I coughed out the last of my air, sucking it back in, clawing around for another weapon. His fist slammed harder than a piston. A wonder a tooth never came loose, then. I clenched that aching jaw on reflex. Another bruise. Grabbing at Barrel's neck distracted him just enough. With the opposite hand, I scraped through the rough turf. Searching. Finding nothing. *Panicking.* Until it practically rubbed my forearm raw. There. Another rock—small, but I could use it. I could fight him. I could win, I knew I could.

Hesitation.

Tristan trampled my wrist and pinned it down. I yelled through the uncontrollable tears, dropped the stone, cried some more. Barrel stood up. They both scowled from above, silent. Couldn't see their faces. Think the only thing I did was turn to my right. Tristan's shoe was scuffed up, laces almost untied—he kicked my chin aside. The blow didn't knock teeth out, either, but they crunched together. I could taste the gash in my tongue. It was over.

"Told you he's crazy," Tristan said at Barrel, who stepped over me as if I'd been dead. I sure felt like it, or wanted to be.

Not a single part of me cared to get back at them. Weak hands. Couldn't try to pull Tristan's ankle if I'd tried. I surrendered that day, and maybe planned to avoid school forever, run from home so my parents wouldn't be able to take me there. Those remained thoughts.

Something in those hits set me straight again. I couldn't fight; I shouldn't have brought anyone to the circle. Mom was right about being stupid, after all.

"I'm sorry I couldn't help you."

Auntie's whisper came from the earth, softly. The tiniest conscience treading on a shoulder.

"You could have hit them back."

"Are you serious?" I remember laying perfectly still. "Tristan's dad is a construction guy—I'd be dead even if I won. And Barry, he's not worth it."

"If you always let others tread over you, they'll never stop."

I rolled toward the circle, spitting a wad of blood into the dirt. My lip was sore. Tears finally came; spoiled as I'd been by long-faded novelties, I had nowhere to go. I looked bashed up and plainly broken. Home would've brought undue judgement. A messy kid was no cause for alarm—Mom and Dad were used to messy—but if they discovered marks of a scuffle, I knew they'd drag me to the teachers for an explanation. And if Tristan testified, I'd be deemed the instigator, no question. That was truer than Auntie's disembodied voice.

"You're not really there, anyway," I'd said while pushing to my feet. "You're not real."

Looming above the hole, I thought its packed-in rocks seemed to quiver, settling before I could blink twice. After a while, she hadn't replied. I left slowly. Every glance over a shoulder had been a nervous tic. I anticipated some retaliation, maybe scolding words or a yell.

As promised, I'd been reprimanded. Not by the voice.

Arriving home around noon hadn't been abnormal, but my mother took me into the living room two steps in the door. She grabbed my dirtied sleeve, pinching it, then started shaking the cloth along with my arm. A small worm jostled out and onto the ground.

Mom scowled in complete horror, kicking the wriggling creature aside. When she'd returned to me, I froze.

"Arthur, what is this? What happened?" she snapped, raising both my forearms. It stung. She inspected the scrapes—I didn't respond quickly enough. "Answer. Now."

I'd told her, "I fell." Unoriginal, I know. There wasn't the time to think it through.

"Fell? Look at all this!"

Directing me by the wrist, upstairs, down the short hallway, she halted near the bathroom. Then pointed at the open door. If only I could forget that expression—lines on her face fiercer than a snarling tiger.

"Clean yourself up," she said, "before your father gets back from work. I don't want him seeing this."

Regressive instinct made the pain emerge sharper, boiling under the surface. Started to cry again because most mothers would've reacted differently.

"We are not throwing a tantrum right now. Go take a bath."

I refused to move, rubbing my eyes with the cleanest parts of my wrists. She didn't leave.

"Arthur Coelho, get moving."

Names were always signaling the last straw. I listened, trudging into the bathroom, without looking behind me. I already knew she'd gone.

The lukewarm stream had rinsed away the smudged, earthy patches, but each and every scrape was too visible, flaking from raw skin. Running water seared against those arms, and my knees weren't much prettier. Upon drying myself, all the injuries stood out, pinkish red, on the light tan I'd acquired from adventuring. It used to be fun. Curiosity had come bearing gifts of wonderful things, the most special an escape I'd rarely gotten elsewhere.

I mulled under the shower until I heard a *splat*. Still had shampoo suds between my fingertips. Though I'd stepped back, looking down, the discolored porcelain-enamel had been bare. Water trickled on my neck. *Squelch.* I tripped forward, turning. It wasn't in front—it was behind, small and unassuming. There was a fleshy, black worm curled up in the bathtub.

If I hadn't already decided to stop lounging in the dirt, I'd made up my mind further. I know I washed that mudworm down the drain.

***

162

Surviving a few lickings and lectures had been par for the course, a middling set of pubescent years. They flew by without leaving me a story to tell; it wasn't novel, just what it was. I suffered a job once I'd gotten permits, and I moved several streets away from my childhood paradise. Suppose it was too difficult to cut ties completely.

For old time's sake, I'd revisited that park long after. I mean *long after*. By about twenty-three, the place became an illusion I'd barely lived with, like an imaginary friend. Nostalgia swelled whenever I drove past on Thanksgiving, but I never imagined I'd see the circle again. It all changed as love softened my willpower—time heals, and time also buries. As much as I forgot the voice, I lost the reason I abandoned it.

Love let me grow up.

High school threw a plethora of work onto my plate, but on the bright side, I met a junior in senior year. Technically, we hadn't talked much until she graduated. We were both straight-C students who earned bountiful careers in fast food; I noticed her, and she recognized me. Things blossomed fast. She started living in my apartment earlier than we expected, all in order to get away from her parents—though I couldn't complain, since I'd moved to avoid mine. Outside the compulsory holiday dinners, life smoothed over.

We hit it off and made it work. Shared rent, shared responsibilities, downtime spent together. Admittedly, there were the quirks. She didn't like nicknames, but granted, Chloe was a name that spoke for itself. Days had her dressing bright and strong like a field of tulips, the cheapest, thriftiest gowns her favorite projects; I bought the new sewing machine she'd wanted, and I didn't wait until Christmas to let her try it out. Just seeing her face turn to sunshine made it worth breaking tradition. Then again, I think we always spoiled each other. Special occasion or not.

Neither of us had the kind of money for excess, though we didn't bother budgeting, not when it came to us. I didn't own many houseplants, only orchids. Chloe bought different colors on her usual whims—the windowsills were never empty. Even learned how to fashion tight knots just so I could hang pots from the ceiling. She might've overestimated how much I enjoyed staring at them. But why would I say no to her? She'd grow terribly worried the more I paid for her hobbies, so I couldn't stop her returning the favors.

It was more than pure generosity. Chloe had an addiction to gifts—giving and receiving. They were kept at an equilibrium. My replenishing of fabrics, threads, and animal-shaped pincushions; her prototype shirts becoming our shared home clothes; inspiration I'd provide through the most innocuous commentary; post-experimenting scraps she'd stitch into neckties. I hadn't considered the process so brittle.

One day, she thought she'd lose the balance forever. I picked up a call from the hospital. Fractured tailbone, the nurse said. Chloe couldn't go back to her job for weeks. She'd taken up arranging displays out-of-town, this chain department store, and if they didn't have the profits to cover the bills, they were lying. I told Chloe to sue—she refused.

"What?" The first word I'd said made her flinch.

"I'm not going to." She wouldn't look at me. "It was my fault. I already called Mom and Dad and they—"

"You *called* them?"

The two people who reminded Chloe she was only as good as her GPA. Every day of her life. They paid for her older brother and sister's college, then complained their youngest was in failing school. She'd amount to nothing. Chloe wouldn't lie about herself, or her parents, or anything, not around me.

I hadn't grown up; I was still naïve.

"Look, nobody else would care," Chloe said. "Least no one in the family."

I couldn't stand hearing her talk that way. "If they already don't, then what are *those two* doing?"

"Paying off the bills..."

"I'll take care of it. Remember? Don't—don't rely on them."

"Then I'd be burdening you."

She looked through me and cried.

I stopped myself.

"If Mom hadn't—" She buried her face in linen. "If I'd never existed—"

"Don't…"

I bandaged Chloe in platitudes even knowing they couldn't heal, much less cover the wounds. Empathy tore at a few of my stitches. I held her hand, comforting myself more than her. *It'd work out.*

She opened her mouth during the silence, not to denigrate herself as I'd anticipated, but to prepare.

"…their dad…I was…"

Didn't know her parents were divorced.

Chloe admitted aloud, "My father…"

… had been the man her mother had an affair with.

It took a trip to the ER to slip out. We'd been together about four years—did she hide it so well, or had I suppressed my instincts? The truth is, I never had them. I was too busy throwing money away.

Yet the boy did have a compass. A voice deep inside resurrected. As I gazed into Chloe's puffy eyes, my mind planted a childish idea. Thumb in the dirt. There was something I forgot—hadn't brought it up to her. Hypocrisy. Funny how everyone has it.

Arguing wore us down, and afterward, I shut the hell up. All I did was promise her something:

"When you're all healed, we're going to the park together."

"The park?" Chloe laughed cautiously. Too hard and she'd hurt herself.

"Yeah," I said. I wove a lengthy tale of the days I'd escaped life, venturing into the broken woods. Where I dug a hole, some special circle, someplace Chloe found too silly for such a reserved man. Couldn't blame her assumptions. I was a stern sort about her wellbeing, a tad overconcerned.

I'll exclude those recovery weeks, however—you'll understand soon.

Cut to the important part. Our date out in that peculiar park had been more a nostalgic trip of my own than a mutual vacation. Save for a few trees guarding the entrance, every plant had grown brittle, brown, and shivered at the slightest shift in the air. I recall an unlatched gate clinking against the fence, its racket fading as our walk led us deeper. *Follow yourself.* My compass seemed adamant, unconscious thing it was.

Metallic tinkling. Shuffling boots. I'd caught those before discovering the man they belonged to.

Blinked my eyes as if I'd been trying to wake up, and he was still there. Officer G dragged a limp leg across the path, a shovel in his hands. Keys rattled at the man's belt. Mud caked his navy uniform; he wasn't wearing the hat, so I'd noticed, curiously, a full head of hair. Perhaps he'd aged well. A silver badge clung to his breast pocket. It was him, all right.

Chloe held my arm tight.

We followed him as a heavy silence drowned the persistent rustling, howling wind leaving us alone with the uniformed man's grating inhales, wheezing exhales. I'm sure now Chloe had been softly asking to turn around and leave, but I couldn't ignore it. The magnetic urge threaded ambition through my legs. Like those days I'd found joy, when I was a kid pushing boundaries. No innate fear could overpower it.

It was her ambiguous vocal twang. Something just close enough to pass for Aunt Theresa, though duller, immersed in even pressure— as if my ears hadn't quite popped.

"You're back. "

The voice tapped a fingernail between my ribs, her memory puncturing the bubble.

"You're back..."

An illusory breeze gathered above our heads, cool and swift, yet soundless. Rushing crosswise in the officer's hair, black sheen flowing on the strands; chills skipped across my skin; Chloe shuddered, too. We were uneasy. Felt as if something in her touch had shared her emotions.

Officer G kept mumbling and pacing around the hole, eyes bloodshot. Some seconds he'd halt in place, coughing until he squealed himself hoarse. His shovel was being clutched with the strength of an apparent rigor mortis, the stiff burden dragging his shoulder down and setting both askew. A ragged line scraped the dirt.

He transfixed us with an uncanny glare; he didn't blink, not once. Mouth ajar, his breathing rattled, the shovel lifting an inch above ground in his trembling grip.

"Kids shouldn't be here," he said with surprising intelligibility. "Oughtta go home, it's gettin' late."

"We *should* go," Chloe whimpered at my side.

After we'd come all this way to see her? I'd thought it rude to leave. Yes, I can't fathom why, but I'd been offended on behalf of the circle.

"Arthur." My woman's arms became demanding, though she was too frail to yank me off balance. "He looks crazy—don't."

I paused a step ahead. "He's not, he's trying to help, I think."

She couldn't have understood, even if I'd spelt it out. Her leg bobbed and kicked forward as she hopped sideways. Staring around her feet, Chloe swore at the earth. Squashing something, smearing it. A black stain was left under her shoe.

"There's one on your ankle!" she yelped.

Dumbfounded, I glanced down. The shoelaces were loose.

Chloe pointed. "There it is, there!"

A chill pierced my nerves to action. I jerked my left leg—tossing a wet, squirming larva off and into the dead grass. Another mudworm tickled the opposite leg, but I leapt before it could perch itself on my foot.

"Arthur—!" Chloe couldn't finish speaking.

My attention rushed from the tip of her finger to where it led.

The officer's hair twisted wildly in thickened clumps; he held as an effigy of rot, breath gone, and eyes rolled back; bitter herbs and unwashed skin made up the rising odor. I witnessed the last of Officer

G's life slip away. His scalp bled profusely as the worms dismounted in a heap; their bodies flailed, thumping onto scoured ground.

I faltered then, unwilling to choose between escape and discovery. Panic was strangely absent. Hundreds of the creatures slithered past, Chloe's footfalls treading dull and rapid behind, growing distant, no louder than her begging for me to run. Why had the worms ignored my legs? Even as the black masses swarmed madly onward, a slew scaling both ankles, each insect plummeted to the dirt without biting. Unlike they'd done to the officer.

His body swelled. I observed—the moment motionless as a snapshot—while a relative calm surfaced from the core, my internal compass yet fixed to the circle. Officer G retched a slop of worms, then collapsed. The shovel toppled with him, yet unreleased from his hand, leaving the arm crooked.

It had taken longer for me to comprehend antipathy than a regular person, or a woman like Chloe. Under the circle's spell, it seemed, I approached the spot I'd known forever.

Mudworms wriggled aimlessly beneath my shoes, some crushed and otherwise maimed as I'd walked across the clearing. The park itself had died while I was busy, its spindly trees and bare bushes painfully shriveled, as if an acid had eaten them from the inside-out, sucking them dry. And where I paused, there was a hole.

Someone had been digging. Tightly packed rocks and dirt once filled the circle; now the shoveled earth was gathered in a mound, just beside the pit. About three-quarters of a foot deep—it couldn't have been more. The hollow space had a messy outline, cracked edges giving it the essence of a madman's midnight toil. No, it wasn't *someone:* it was the officer. He'd done this.

I knew how, but not why. I hadn't dared to ask aloud. Didn't need to when she'd heard everything.

"Such a helpful man." Her voices buried their needling words in my skin. "Arthur, I'm happy you've come to your senses. It's good to see you, dear."

She wasn't Aunt Theresa.

If I had the ability to shut out her call, I would—I'd have shut the door to my head and barricaded it. But lacking the will, I suffered the murmurs, the trepidation, as I rejected every slight inclination of hers outright. As she spoke in solemn groans, my hands took up the shovel in the officer's grasp. His mass laid prone. Resolute even beyond death.

I yanked at the tool's splintering handle.

She delivered wistful phrases, manipulating Auntie's tone as if she'd been above, below, and everywhere.

"Should the..."

I didn't hear them; the officer's fingers held. Surely, I'd grown, hadn't I? Wasn't I strong enough?

"...light within..."

The shovel appeared to dislodge, but upon tugging again, I couldn't pull it further. I'd cursed at my hands—stress weakened them. Losing to a corpse was less than dignifying. I fought with the officer's arm until it hurt, both my palms burned raw.

"Follow...and..."

It came free. It came free and I caught myself teetering back, befuddled in momentary triumph. Courage lifted me, impulse set my arms in motion, and resentment kept them working.

"...return to..."

Dust and debris cluttered the air while I shuffled soil into the shallow circle. The more I covered it, the more she suffocated—the more her voices screeched and wailed their dissonant displeasure. Frostbite nipped my chest.

I was brought to tears. I'd known she wasn't the real one, but it felt all too sincere when she'd said she loved me. Even as I'd buried her in that hole of muddy depression. Even if she'd left without me.

Ignoring cold and the surging anguish, one exertion after another, I'd thrown dirt over the circle. Only sunrise could end my insanity.

***

Perhaps the world—no, *family* brought loneliness, but in my thirties, I discovered what it meant to be alone. A decade melded into a period shorter than a passing year. Seemed it did.

My hobbies hadn't changed, and neither did my career. Maybe I'd changed jobs, but none of them exhausted me. It had gotten simpler as I adapted; mornings to afternoons were reserved for work, and the nights were mine alone. Data entry wasn't the most respectable label on my resume, just a practical choice. Made no difference so long as I could pay rent.

Went to the park each night, sitting beside the circular mound, and I listened to her muttering. She didn't speak to me anymore. Instead, the vocal pollution overlapped itself, picking similar words to those I'd ignored years ago. Not that I'd paid better attention.

Chloe had moved on and out shortly after we'd visited the park together. Understandably, she likely couldn't face the man who'd abandoned her. And watched distantly as another died before his eyes. I'd pretend I never cared for her in the first place, though, unambiguously, it was a lie. Wherever I looked—ceiling, counters, windowsill—the potted orchids reminded me she'd left.

At some point, I neglected the flowers more than my body. They wilted in no particular order. So, I'd taken a spade to them, trashing the plants and musty soil, but leaving the pots intact as I waxed hopeful, dreaming of buying new bulbs or cultivating something else. To no one's surprise, I didn't do either.

I've never moved those stacked pots from the kitchen counter. Couldn't throw them away—I feel queasy passing them. They'll evoke the happiest moments of my life, if I'm in a nostalgic mood. Reminiscing hasn't been pleasant lately. For every second I'd savor pleasure, there were twice the unwanted memories to stomp out the flames. Then and now, now and then. Doesn't matter if it's today or the man at thirty-three.

I paused. The realization settled one day, age thirty-eight, when I'd been months deep undoing my regrets. A spade in hand, and many, many books sprawled on the coffee table. Of geology, gardening, survival, death—especially the biological process of death. I'd propped up a guide to local pests on the spine of a medical textbook.

Nauseating ideas seeped in as the universe slowed. I couldn't have been myself. From the time I lost contact with Chloe until that evening; years hazy under an ordinary schedule; somehow, in a bout of sobriety, I wrote the procedure down. It was maddening. Waking and driving to work; eating, though not often; drinking tap water, forgetting to buy a filter, tasting the sourness of the city; but most importantly, I'd spent every evening at the park. I clenched the spade's handle. She didn't relent—I didn't notice I had dug up the hole again.

No, it wasn't only that. Shelving the books, I took to the closet for my coat, boots, and a hat—it was about the same time of year. Officer G's body had vanished, but I hadn't been aware since she...damn, I really wasn't myself. There was a connection to her. Always *her*. I stuffed the spade in my belt and hurried out the door.

As expected, I came upon the clearing as before: deserted, dehydrated, and embracing the distorted circle. But in my restored awareness, I couldn't describe the sunken spot as a mere hole. It was a chasm. Only a few steps into the sanctuary, and she swallowed the path. I blinked some hallucination. Officer G had fallen several feet ahead—yes, right there, he'd ...

I held my eyes open. Below, a ring of mushrooms surrounded the abyss, right at its edges. They were the liveliest things I'd ever seen. Plump, sprinkled with condensation. Unassuming. Content. The only growths to survive where grass hadn't sprouted for several seasons—stunning persistence. A cloud of breath fogged over my reading glasses; I'd forgotten I'd been wearing them.

"Follow the end..."

Something—someone brushed against my wrist. Dainty, familiar hands clasped around one of mine. Though I meant to glance, Chloe's smitten eyes led me aside. They had a color I instantly compared to dead leaves. An unflattering metaphor, but their shade of brown suited the crumbling glade.

How right I'd been.

"Follow the end." Chloe smiled. So, she *had* said it after all.

Her wide pupils seemed evocative; they deepened the pit in my gut, and, implicitly, I'd looked to the chasm.

Chloe shifted, playing a dangerous game. Toes at the edge. Arms anchored by me and nothing else.

"Wait," I said, breathless, "Chloe, you can't."

She let go, happy as always; she began to fall; but I'd grabbed her by the forearm, squeezing it. And heard a squelch.

"You can't!" I held her anyway. Things were very, very wrong.

A black worm poked out from her ear, then her other. Lesions spread across Chloe's paling skin.

"Come here," she spoke through unmoving lips, balancing her feet on the perimeter. I tightened my grip. "Help us, I know you've wanted to."

"Stop using her, you selfish—!"

Chloe slipped as I yelled—mudworms burst from her spotted wounds. If I'd tried to catch her, I would've plummeted headfirst into Hell.

I couldn't give that circle the satisfaction.

Even the heartless can cry; I like to think I'd been sadder about almost dying than losing Chloe. Didn't need anyone. Humans aren't immortal, nobody's worth the sacrifice. Those mantras uphold an egocentric preservation.

Well, the abyss wouldn't require my help anymore, would it? I'd pulled the spade from my belt, offering it to the circle. Endless shadow devoured the glint of the blade.

My humble gardening tool fell and fell, and it never landed.

***

Forty-nine years old. Newsmen babbled on as the sinkhole pervaded media attention, local networks unable to resist causing panic. Where I remained, the apartments suffered too many apathetic people. Nobody believed the whispers in the television static. In fact, while the city's sheltered and wealthy began evacuation, we were liberated by disaster.

Our debts wouldn't matter once we died. But I'd made up my mind—live a bit longer, watch the Earth disappear.

When autumn soon shut its curtain, the sinkhole hesitated, as if the script cued a dramatic beat. The news ate it up.

"An unprecedented natural phenomenon...with origins in Atlantic City, sinkholes have been reported across the county...but expert geologists point to related cases in the tri-state area as a sign of...dangerous times ahead. President...citizens are outraged at the sparse emergency response..."

I laughed at the screen. TV hadn't entertained me this much since I was a boy, and it didn't then, either.

Luckily, alcohol subdued the constant resonance from the living chasm. Despite living a safe distance away, she'd convene in my head—no permission given, naturally. She should've stuffed me with mind-control worms, I suppose, if she didn't want me to drink her into silence.

Sleep had been a struggle. Before I routinely nursed myself on the finest Bordeaux, each night, I'd toss and turn, hearing things, words—psychic phrases. Her chorus peeled away sanity faster than a flood ruined drywall. Wine solved that. I wasn't so much glad as I was relieved, maybe a touch more exhausted once I could be.

After several glasses, the bed would soothe my worries. Few downsides to the method, actually. Consequent dreams were either vividly distorted or completely dark, which I didn't mind, and I often forgot them in the morning.

I have a reason to mention these dreams—albeit an incongruous topic on its face—because I'd written one drunken sequence down, the original entry so impeccable, I've copied it verbatim below. Some additions were required, but I haven't smoothed all the creases.

I believe the best comes from its crude construction:

As most dreams started, I sank through the mattress. Falling often paradoxically drags the body heavily, and yet it floats on air, especially when the scenery fades to black. I assume it's not uncommon.

It drenched my senses with an ocean current—in no time, it drained from the atmosphere. Still visionless, I made to shift an arm, or a leg, but to no avail. My neck was likewise fixed in place. Surrendering, I allowed the mind to perform freely.

A hitched breath implied I'd made a mistake. Dread pushed my torso upward, holding me in a seated position; I couldn't speak. But as I'd lost my nerve, an aquamarine light gleamed overhead.

White soon engulfed the softening blues.

I'd called it welcoming at first, though looking around, I gradually retracted that acceptance. Optical illusions accentuate the abnormal. Once they twist too far, it becomes impossible to mistaken their deception. I wasn't a gullible child anymore.

The room was a bit too wide and long to perceive at once. With time, every discovery complicated further. Walls traveled endlessly in the cardinal directions there, and I couldn't make out a doorway from those shadowed depths at the ends. No corners to speak of, I thought, until the lacking light gave it equal parts angularity and roundness. I'd observed as the room swelled and shrunk in diaphragmic undulation. Not a single crumbling emission from the brickwork encasing the burrow. No sound louder than the voice narrating discomfort, despite the expectation of such from a moving, living void. I gulped its bitter air. It seemed an illusion. False if not for my vision yet capturing it. I was no hypocrite—if I believed in things I've heard and never seen, I couldn't discount what I did see but would never hear.

Then, I heard. For its first echo, it breathed out an alluring perfume to match the words:

"I've missed you, kiddo." With a sugary flavor finding its way into my mouth.

And in tandem, another said, "I missed you," nothing more.

Both were higher pitched, but the former had a characteristic rasp. Auntie. Coughing up something solid, I spat the taste to the dirt. A glossy hard candy, cherry red—she'd buy them in packs for me when my mother wouldn't. They'd been my favorite. *Auntie hadn't forgotten.*

Tart, freezing crystals melted under my tongue, the ceiling frosting over unnaturally. Icicles grew rapidly downward, starting at the room's edges, sprouting in a wave toward me, crackling as if they'd snap instantly. But they expanded. They hissed and dug deep into the now moistening dirt underneath—their advance halted without warning. Encircling me. If only the beauty in their symmetry could have soothed the oncoming pains.

I lurched forward, just short of curling into a ball. When my head bowed some inches to greet shaking knees, the motion froze over—I'd frozen over. I'd begun choking on ice rising from my very core and coating the ridges of my palate, tongue seized by stabbing rime. I'd been unable to scream beyond my mental prison.

An opaque white crystalized below, binding both legs to the surrounding mud. I sank. Slowly, but certainly, I plunged into a disgusting cold, wet, clingy, squelching heap absorbing skin and clothing alike. Its filth oozed through the garments—anything on my person—making them stick uncomfortably to crevices where I'd have never wanted raw earth.

The improbability of it all struck me as my chin submerged. So I'd believed in the fantastical—did it matter? This wasn't real—it was utterly pointless—I'd suffered the method acting of the brain in slumber. I knew so from the sudden shift in my posture. Hunched as I was, I'd simultaneously felt my spine straight, back laid against a firmer, cottony support. In both positions—impossible. It was one or the other, not both.

But the dream threatened to supersede reality, prove itself in the face of my denial. Frost engulfed me until it burned. The earth still pulled my agreeable body into its suffocating embrace. Mud seeped through my lips in spite of their tight closure. Then filling nostrils and ears. I shut both eyes in reflex—in primal fear. No air. The ground rose to my hairline—rather, my hairline disappeared as I surrendered to the ground. No air. Gasping proved disastrous—it sucked mud through desperate nostrils, into deprived airways.

"Stop kidding yourself."

I awakened to winter's first snow; a wonder lost on a heart recovering from night terror. Admiring the closest window pane, I let myself think. Whispering winds. A branch tapping at the glass. Young birds faintly pestering their mother. Peace exhaled, and I inhaled. Altogether it rinsed the worrisome parts off my mind.

I'd forgotten to turn the heater up.

For all you know, I began yesterday. A morning to write, an evening to publish, and today you've come across the journal. Unbelievable, you'd cry. But you have no proof I exist. And I can't be certain you're reading, or have read everything I've had to say. I suppose I could've shortened this considerably. In fact, several yesterdays ago, I'd drafted a list representing the timeline, though its inadequacy led me to undertake an accurate, unabridged record.

... Even there, I've failed. Time is growing bothersome; enduring it seems useless, now. Whether these final pages survive alone or all of them scatter into the wind, once I've finished writing, I'll break free of the ground. She's tempted me for too long.

She says she cares, she'll do anything to keep me happy. Making excuses for herself. I tell her every now and then that I'd be happier if she let go, but we're both trapped beyond time and space. The world is gone. Her void calls and whines beneath my home. A single spire supports this battered apartment; my neighbors above and below had been drawn into the abyss one by one, jumping from their windows, several hitting the cliffs before dropping into her welcoming eternity. They didn't scream. They fell peacefully, eyes blackened where their whites should've been. I could watch and do nothing. By then, I'd regarded them as vacantly as a thunderstorm. It was inevitable they'd pass.

The mudworms had infested their heads—I'd imagine the creatures burrowed in when the calamity first gnawed at the earth. I've managed to dissect a hand-caught specimen once, but discovered nothing. They were just worms. Could a simple pest cause mankind's collective apathy? I've been offered their mercy, and I can't determine why. They crawl over my foot as if I'm furniture. Shouldn't they devour me all the same?

She tells me they're her friends; they aren't going to hurt me.

I appreciate the honesty. Most humans defer blame to others instead, but a being like her never does—well, I may be wrong. She's said nobody else was meant to find her. If I'd sated her appetite decades earlier, she'd cease to exist and become freed from herself. What a joke. As if I'm to blame for the end of the world. She's not Aunt Theresa at all; she's probably my mother.

People fed to her become her, in theory. Had my parents fled the city early, they would've delayed their fall, not prevented it. The void may think she's done me a favor, purging them. She may consider me elated to have freedom from their verbal and mental plague. She's right. I've wished ill upon my biological parents since the day my father took to the bottle. I'm no treasure, but she's hardly earned obedience from that stunt alone.

She explains she's essentially killed the problems at their roots. Pesticide damages beyond its intended targets, however; she's poisoned her fate. I have nowhere to run, and she couldn't run to begin with.

Assuming the planet is capsized, everything must be devastated—if I haven't been found. Humanity boasts a history where being crafty signifies survival, quality of life aside. Helicopters would've arrived if the abyss halted in a ring around my apartment. Similarly, if I'd gone insane, someone would've woken me. If I were dead, this hell is tame. Too dull.

Had I angered a fickle god, perhaps in a past life? Why me? Isn't this what I'm meant to question? *Why me?* To punish the Earth for one man's stubbornness—I can't describe the divine lesson I'm undergoing. I ...

She's whispering. She hasn't stopped since...it's strange, but her voices are clearer. They're blending and fading while the words come to me: *a light within.* More, more of them. One voice. Not a choir, no. I don't know who she's emulating now; the pitch is too balanced and the throat sounds unscathed by age or vices.

Here she is.

Should the suffering whelp grace Her plane,

He perceives a light within his pain;

Follow the end and so she'll entrust

That none but He shall return to dust.

Always about destiny, how I'm at fault. It's my fault. *It's your fault...* . No. It isn't. Who does she think she is—who I am? Get out of my head! It's done! I have it ready, I'm winding the last knot. I am *leaving* if you push.

Writing and thought are corrupted by her, but she has a timid side. You see, I've been tying myself a sturdy rope in the meantime, and she's rather desperate to lead me off the edge, pathetically so. She's ingested the world, yet a single, mortal man reduces her to this toothless noise.

It *is* a joke, I know it. Fate bestowed the birthright of sacrifice on a man. Not merely a road to enlightenment through selflessness, no, instead the capitulation which brings a greater good—; for the world, I'm everything and nothing; but I realize how foolish they are, these higher powers I point to in vague accusation. They should know of freewill. I can disobey—I *will* cause them trouble. Shouldn't they have solved this themselves, if they'd cared? But the possibility exists for their apathetic whims and subsequent entertainment garnered at my expense, I wager. Granted, as well, they've no obligation to preserve us. If they created the calamity, her prison, and the key to unlock it, they'd been sadistic from the beginning of the universe.

God, I'm terrified. I wrote to stall my own solution, and in reward I've gotten shakier hands. Softer knees, mentally chained ankles...cold feet. Figurative language does hold some validity. Physically, I've never experienced the frigid nerves as psychosomatic. Rather, they came with the wintertime, then summer would melt the emotions off my faces. Inside, I'd calmed; outside, I'd warmed.

Deep breaths help. They help a little, I think, if I can control my hands. The closing knot fought the whole way through, but I've tightened it. A firm one. Unused nooses are piled beside my bed, their ropes frayed or partly undone. It isn't as if I couldn't. I grew confident I'd never need them—I'd outlive her, ignore her abyss forever, maybe die of old age. *Fifty more years!* I thought, *fifty has taken damn well forever already!* I'd looked over the cliff once a day. She couldn't win; I vowed to end the world's quarrel.

My record will survive me, so please, at least pay it a glance. Though I—I shouldn't be asking favors of the unknown. After what she's wrought from the Earth, I should be grateful if the ink doesn't fade. Will she finally consume the apartment to get me? It doesn't matter. I'll never offer my body—she'll have to take it herself, shamefully.

You don't blame me, I hope. I don't know you—if you're alive, you're certainly not from around here. It likely matters little that I'm responsible for anything, let alone everything falling apart. I'm sure you'll forget once it's over. Forgive this man's godly coup d'état.

The hooks in the ceiling bear a lengthy rope, taut strings looping above and around my bedroom. May the fringed end hold its knot. I'll say a farewell to the stacked pots on the counter, then I can rest easy; without the orchids, I wouldn't have drilled those hooks up there. Thank you. If Chloe hadn't been so generous, I...I love you, dearly. I'm grateful you aren't alive to stop me—but it wouldn't work if you did. Sorry I've been stubborn.

She's yelling. She can neither force me to chase destiny, nor reject the routes I take without her. What's the matter? Silence, puckering silence. I'll die satisfied if she's gotten even the tiniest bit angry. Or if she's pricked by the barb of remorse. My mother would writhe in disdain, my father no different, and Aunt Theresa...

Shut up, shut up, *shut up, stop, I—*

I've set the chair, shut the blinds, and made the bed; worms gather around my feet; well, I wonder if they're expecting my humble insubordination. They aren't aggressive. She hasn't quit her damned shrieking, yet. Some abyssal being she is, throwing tantrums, wailing like a banshee. Imagine a world where she can't be freed by a man's death—where she's trapped for eternity, only herself to blame. Blissful. No hesitation. I can imagine it, and I'm going to create this paradise alone.

I refuse to fall into her open grave.

She had been bound at her wrists, hung from the sky, and left alone.

The rope was pulling apart thread by thread.

"Beginning," she said. "It's the beginning."

All she felt was the ache of longing for someone.

Then, the rope snapped.

In One Glance

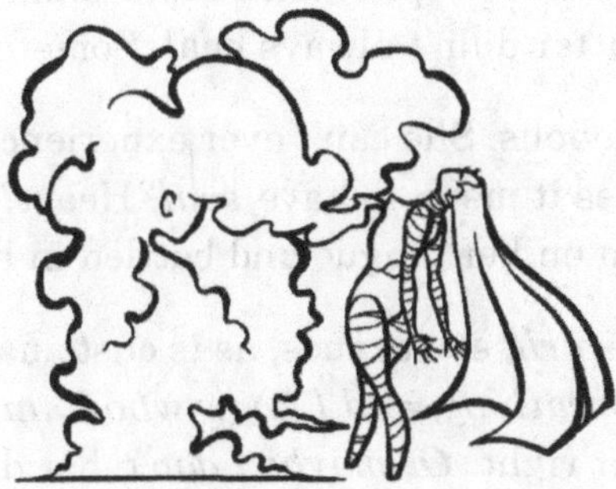

The heart knows what it wants, and the head doesn't like it. Walk out the front door beyond midnight, taste the rain that isn't there; she has a thought she can't verbalize. She's been here before, awake. A light on the porch ahead of her shouldn't be on, she knows it, because no one lives in the neighborhood. This isn't home. She's crossed into another again.

Pleasance blinks her real world to life, grassland on a finite island floating in the sky. Running a leg—bandaged into a spike and no natural footing—across the cliff, she kicks a pebble off, where it descends forever. At birth, she'd tried to fling herself toward the eternal blue, but The Clouds carried her to the island with a stubborn windstorm. Nearly stubborn as her. She smiles despite a smothered mouth, thinking through nostalgia; she's different than she had been.

Two marble pedestals stand two paces behind her, the empty one more comfortable for her elbow. She steps back to prove just this, leans onto the flat surface, then reconsiders the spot. It's solid, supports well enough. The *opposite* of comfy. For a miserable second, Pleasance endures it. Then she fidgets away from the pedestal, straightens her back. Boredom does make her aware of and prone to doing the stupidest things.

Admiring left, to the broken ceramic bust, Pleasance tugs at her facial wrappings. Nervous habit, of course, but she does mean to pull the golden cloth down this time. She stops at her tightly swathed neck, the exact breaking point on the other sculpture. The Clouds toys with the direction of the wind. Her lips run cold as her neck wound tingles. *But can I call it one?* She isn't positive she can, if she's made of baked clay. It isn't possible to hurt material things. Realms outside her own had people with

182

skin and bone and warm, rushing blood pumped into veins by a beating muscle. A counterpart she'd met said it was a *heart*. That hearts were important whether physical or spiritual. People could suffer injuries of either heart, but the latter didn't always heal. Sometimes it never would.

Pleasance is envious. She can't ever experience a physical heart, and a soul . . . what does it mean to have *soul?* Heart? The words are lovely; she usually keeps them on her tongue and bottled in her head.

I must have a spirit, she argues, as is customary every few hours. *I'm thinking without breathing, and I know who I am.* Pleasance dusts off the bare pedestal to her right. *Or maybe I don't,* her distraction goes. *Doesn't matter.* Existential questioning is all a woman can have if nothing changes, so she believes. Repositioning her bandages, Pleasance takes a brief stroll south, where the island's center is marked by a limestone circle. The pedestals and the circle are all she's ever seen—in terms of manmade things. Although, there's a second complication. They aren't manmade either.

The Clouds laughs, as if his safety above permits reading her thoughts. She hates when he does.

Come down here, then! Pleasance poses atop the center, gazing upward.

A wispy cluster playfully sails across, growing larger, soon covering the blue and leaving her in shade.

She pulls down the wrappings in a huff. He doesn't listen, but she wouldn't love him if he did. Pleasance keeps her attention above, pointing at the broken sculpture. "Aren't you going to tell me who the other one is? You promised!"

"I didn't promise," The Clouds says. He isn't lying—she knows he hadn't made a vow, though she's exhausted most excuses to pry the story from him.

Unfortunate the plan fails so easily and slips between her fingers, or else she'd get somewhere closer to an answer. Pleasance regrets trying to understand The Clouds, to interrogate him, to be enslaved to pregnant pauses as he withholds his truths; neither of them are like humans, but they act too similarly for Pleasance to find peace in blind faith. To act

183

human and be inhuman—it's called anthropomorphizing when a person does it. Can she give herself something she isn't?

"You're too infatuated with objective truth, that's your problem," The Clouds groans, swirling around Pleasance. He makes a ring of himself. "Can't you let us exist in the absence of complications? You're the only one worried."

"I'm not worried," she bites.

"It's written on your face. Your eyes are worse than foglamps."

"How do you know what foglamps are?"

"The dream you had of those cars—you said what they were."

"I didn't. I was someone else then."

The Clouds whips over, gathering his form; he descends with the silhouette of a man in formal wear, landing on the limestone, his left foot forward and intercepting the ground; not a clatter from the airy figure, unlike a real body; he turns to her sidelong while giving a cocky tilt of his head. The cumulonimbus makes up hair, billowing long past his waist as a grayish, woolen clump. But he remains a cloud, or many, and Pleasance remains a former statue. A vapor, a solid.

She smiles when he does, which leads him to slouch.

"Can you tell who I am, now?" he asks.

Pleasance taps her chin. "You're you."

"No, try guessing again."

This is infuriating. It hasn't been a minute. "I don't know. What do *you* have to do with me being someone else?"

"Nothing. I just thought you'd like me this way."

Very infuriating.

"Humans are more annoying, I think. I don't understand why you're concerned with being one." He pretends to pat her shoulder, miming just so it doesn't pass through. "Besides, you keep your actual body here."

Pleasance withdraws, clasping her satin hands together. "It has sentimental value, is all. I'd . . . "

The Clouds raises a finger. "Would never do it, Pleasance."

"Whaaaat?" she whines.

"You've asked too many times and worn out your chances."

"Then tell me a—"

"Worn out that one, too."

"Stop finishing my thoughts!" She stomps the pointed bandages to no intimidating noise. "Let me talk!"

"Fine, fine." The Clouds shrugs.

Embarrassingly, Pleasance takes back fighting for verbal space. What can be said? He's omniscient to the point of invading privacy, meaning her insight is a one-way connection, while his can and will be fuller than clumped, foggy hair. Not a fair deal for breaking one's own neck.

"You're easy to read, not much to it," The Clouds fibs terribly.

"I don't believe you. You have some sort of ability, sir, and I'm not letting you win each time I open my mouth!"

"But you certainly hesitate to shut it."

"Powderhead!"

"Name-calling, how very *Pleasance*."

"Airbrain!"

"I'd rather have your ability," he shifts the subject, puffing another laugh. "If I had eyes, I'd weave the finest fabrics, not those superficial things."

His slackened hand motions toward her outfit.

"They aren't . . . superficial," she says and hopes he doesn't hear, "I love them . . . and—"

Bemused, she pinches the light blouse, tugging from the chest. Below are rounded shorts, tied by a cotton cord—loose as walked-through shoelaces—the pants covering her hips, and sporting pillowy sides. She admires the ruffled trim at the bottom. There had been nothing inauthentic about gifts from The Clouds.

The clothing is nearly stifling, but exhilarating. She's wearing him. Because he refuses to replace her body, the surface is it; he won't give more. Pleasance may start crying. Perhaps a fickle presence like The Clouds denies her happiness to forgo a lover's responsibility, afraid to lose her, or he prefers their shared freedom. They were brought to the same world by chance, not a divine mistake.

He folds his mouth into an unusual pout for but a second. Wandering off a step, The Clouds crouches lower, sitting on the center's edge. Legs crossing at the calves. Closing himself in posture as he falsely studies the sky-blue expanse surrounding them. Pleasance weaves her cloth fingers together, shuddering. His hair builds a mound behind him, mist pouring onto the limestone and flowing past her legs and possibly even through the grass.

Pleasance blinks a sudden sleepiness from her eyelids—she covers the yawn. But it is noisy.

"You've learned it from them," The Clouds remarks.

"It comes naturally when I see you," she admits with a cheery tone.

"Do I bore you?"

"No, no, no!" How stupid of him. "They call it an empathetic response."

"I'm daygazing. What is to be empathized with?"

She regards the pedestals, eyeing the marble base. Shaped as a symbol—a heart, each relic post in a half-chamber. Spinning on one leg, Pleasance hums, mentally counting the compass-like arrangement of the grounded hearts.

One. North and South have their points directed to the center. "I enjoy daygazing, too," she chirps.

"You'll enjoy anything if I do it."

Two. East and West are built inversely, compared with the other symbols, bestowing the island its harmonious symmetry. "I will not."

The Clouds abruptly cuts their chat short again.

Three. She balances, arms postured like a chevron. East, South, and West's marble hearts are somewhat smaller than North; North is where the pedestals are. Falling past them takes her to the best places when she's unconscious. *They're both empty if I wake in the dream,* she twirls, head stopping at the pedestals. *Why is that so?*

Pleasance gasps, catching the loosened bandages—her body was pirouetting by itself. She hastily looks down. It's her spine—she's the wrong way. For once she remembers her glasses. They fall, bounce off the center stage, then land in safe, dewy grass.

Without a sound, her spectacle frames are caught in The Clouds' hair. They disappear from whence they came.

"Pardon, sir!" Pleasance turns too quickly at the neck, setting her head free of its wrappings. She spouts quite an uproar. All this because she'd refused to secure them around her skull—but accidents hadn't happened since she'd first bound the dressings. This is an unlucky day.

Clovers and weeds squish beneath her, most certainly sticking to the lengthy hair she doesn't tie up. She can taste them, these sprouts of earth, their dirtying her well-combed masterpiece, inhaling their pungent scent. Bitter and inedible. Once again, some cruel reminder; as Pleasance is inhuman, so too is the hair on her head. Acting as keratin follicles while having properties of wet clay, much to her inconvenience.

Pleasance can only change herself as far as this. To mimic, and not *be.* She gazes upon the golden, bandaged legs of her currently headless body, which is frozen without a head to guide it. The cloth slips.

It'll fall apart! A speechless mouth. She is too busy whimpering, tears unfolding from her in ribbons, piling onto the grass.

"You aren't human." The Clouds disperses, immersing the island's surface in a hazy film. But he avoids touching her head. "You're meant for the earth itself."

Quaking, unraveling, the imitation body drops to the center stone. A heap of satin remains—her sculpture lands on it in one piece. Grateful as she is, it's a contradictory assessment. Reflexes are powerless to sway the wet cement drying atop this pitiful hope. Sorrow without faith means grief, more bottomless than the floating island's sky. *Selfish, selfish tears,* she bawls, *to care more of myself than The Clouds. He values this place. He values us. Stop it.* Gilded fabric still escapes her eyes, the discarded wrappings swept into the air along with the newborn tears, soon building together, thrashing as flags caught in a headwind. They fly where she can no longer follow, straight upward. Sculptures have no muscles, no movement; they have no heart.

I don't have a spirit. Pleasance stops thinking in speech altogether. It's decided.

"You shouldn't allow who you are to cause you pain," The Clouds rumbles, grimace unseen but envisioned behind those words. "Whether in your own body or walking in another's shoes, saying right or wrong things, doing good or bad, or anything between. When all returns here, you are yourself. And you're alone."

"I'm with you," she utters hasty and unrefined.

"You're alone. Don't lie about how you feel."

"You took him from me." The island shivers, feeling nothing but a nudge. Pleasance grates her jaw. She isn't sobbing anymore. It had ceased abruptly, at will. "You could've saved him."

"What makes you so sure of someone you've spoken not a word to?" Thick atmosphere, evidence of his opposition.

"It's jealousy on your part. Pure jealousy."

"Childish."

"You saved me, but let him drop endlessly into your skies, until the winds flaked his skin, he fell and spun madly, and then dissolved the way minerals blend through scalding water."

"Childish, ignorant girl."

Pleasance stares. They're pecking a hairline crack into a planet. She forces a grin, though the world is bittering her tongue.

Their island suffers a tremor too great for its size—heaving the blue horizon in its wake, impossibly. But only implausible by the conventions of human life. She realizes the confusion had been her own fault; she'd lulled herself into the dreams and mindscapes of them, her beloved vessels, her people, her ideals, hers, *hers.*

She doesn't give a damn about an answer right now. It's exhausting.

"Don't you dare sleep, I'm talking to you."

To The Clouds, Pleasance offers her final defiance. Another realm finds her inner eyelids, a sweltering wasteland welcoming, begging her to explore forever in a minute. Just like every dream.

***

Sand shuffles, rolls, throws itself across earth pocked with holes and shattered by persistent dryness, an aromatic wind carrying pig's flesh on its howls. There is nothing for miles. Impossible to see a mile's distance, normally, but the inclination of curiosity draws the world back. She finds herself shrinking, and she scans the desert from above. Confirming an unwelcome suspicion, a speck lies ahead of her vessel. As she dives, seeking the body, the sanctity of human skin, her perspective holds on a particular detail: how homely this girl looks. Her face is flushed and shining; she perspires in droplets, but she seems unbothered, snub nose inhaling calmly despite the dusty wind. She's wearing two-piece swimwear, bright orange—a futile effort against the sun. Bowed knees, weak ankles. No sense of figure, feminine by the shape in her eyes—proportionally large, doeish irises—their lashes an appealing length. Pleasance drops to the surface just in front of the idle girl. Lines scour the vessel's features.

Pleasance steps into the body, assuming it. The rays seep through and burn.

Pain is human. She has no energy to smile at the dumbness within herself. She must walk forward.

Sandal prints build behind her, scuffing the ground each step toward that alluring destination. She looks down and listens to the shuffling feet. *I've always forgotten them.* When tying her bandages, the upper body had seemed more vital. Hands and arms the most. They created, maintained, and destroyed closer to the heart. What good were legs for other than the silhouette? The heaviness in this dreamer's feet soon nettles Pleasance. *Unnecessary things.* She rather prefers the sky—touching the earth reminds her of how anchored she really is. *I've never needed them.* But they were human. Humans had hands and arms and legs and feet. Limbs, a plural. Extremities.

189

She licks her lips, tasting grit. Looking up, she follows a glint from her right. The frame of a dilapidated car—missing tires, its rims crushed; torn driver's seat, the foam pouring from a gash, headrest gone; steering wheel bent, grips bubbling and peeling, exposed metal rusted—all sitting in the direct sunlight. Pleasance hunches cautiously, knowing a man resides on the passenger side.

He lifts his head while he fumbles around the glove compartment. Sky blue staring at her. Frayed hair, dirty blond, tied back at the nape of his neck. A drenched shirt clings to him, chest heaving, the cloth hiking up the side of his torso.

She takes the shambled driver's seat, and she sighs. "I made it," Pleasance says.

"Took you forever," the man replies, hiding something in his hand. "Not too comfortable, is it?"

"It's a wreck," Pleasance agrees. An unexpected breeze cools the skeletal cabin, though the next minute heats up again. She shifts from his face to his hand—hand to face. "What'd you find?"

He beams handsomely. "Oh, you'll like it."

"Show me, show me."

"Close your eyes."

In a dream? She wouldn't dare risk blinking to somewhere else. Or back home.

"Please show me, go on!" she insists, her shoulder sidling along toward his.

He laughs softly, quite briefly, burning cheeks caught in the grin. His forehead, baked red from the outside, creases with a raised brow, some guilt on him like a boy who'd just told a terribly obvious lie. The sun shines on through the shattered windshield.

She sticks to him.

His hand opens, and resting on his palm is a single chocolate, its foil untarnished and unbroken.

"It's all that's left." He offers it to her. "You take it."

Pleasance gently picks up the sealed confection, holding it as he did, and she hesitates, glancing to him for certainty. He nods, rather a quick lift of his chin.

"Um . . ." Just pitiful. She can't accept the sweet so selfishly—she won't indulge alone. *What if . . . ?* Pleasance is generous. But to share this, why, it would be a *vulgar* trade. Chilled from the hand, she merely observes the wrapper. It is the coldest thing in this world. Soothing enough to overcome the searing heatwaves.

Pleasance watches the man's lips. *Neither of us needs to go without.*

The gift drops back into his hand; he seems at ease. Resplendent is everything he is to her. She won't partake without him.

And a realm like this moves fortune at her whim.

The man peels the wrapper off, crushing it in his other hand before discarding it; he glances over during the bite. Pleasance doesn't breathe. He holds the uneven half of chocolate hostage, its melted center trickling onto his thumb, and he doesn't chew his portion, keeping his mouth shut. Smiling.

She obtains the rest from him when he offers once more, and she does so willingly, placing the softened candy on her tongue. Copying him.

Savoring it takes patience, waiting for the outer shell to surrender itself as the center does, oozing into her palate, between the finest crevices in her teeth, slowly seducing tastebuds with rich, milky cocoa—which may as well be pure sugar to her. She's never tasted so vividly as different persons, in different places.

In her gluttony, Pleasance swallows. *Ah. Didn't want to yet.* While crawling, struggling, stumbling over the gearshift, she bumps her head on the roof—torn, light slipping through two large slivers—but the clumsy motion doesn't hinder much.

Silent, the man pretends the nothing outside is worth observing. He nearly gulps.

Don't. Pleasance backs him into the broken door, anxious that it will shove open. But it holds their weight as if it were a wall. Fortunate again.

He leers at her eyes, then a touch lower, settling back—a position entirely unnatural for the front seats. His hands don't bother waiting to grab her hips.

A fever hits; but she shivers, pressing her arms onto his chest.

Pleasance isn't the type to separate quantity from quality—she takes as much as he gives, stealing the running confection from his mouth once, and several times over. Chocolate soon becomes indistinguishable from honey. All sugar to her. They cavort without any doubt or distance, though she admits, the taste is fuller on his tongue.

***

"Do you still desire a human heart?"

The Clouds is her mattress, pillow, and blanket, bundled around her and warming. He doesn't leave much room for a decision, adding, "After all of that, do you?"

"They aren't real dreams. You've found out how to make them, too," mouths Pleasance—he'll hear even the weakest voice of hers.

"Don't be daft."

"You want me to be myself, you hate what I love, that I want to love. That isn't love."

"Come now, neither of us can define love. Your dreams have naught to do with me. I never keep you from them, I don't make them."

"It's so disgusting," she says—listlessness is the worst of her might, surfacing when she's given in; "you've had to have made me do those things."

"If I loved you—"

"I don't like you anymore. You're not fun."

Thunder rolls. His thickening mist grows to greater heights, converging above, blocking out the blue and daylight. A cage with no bars, perhaps to threaten her; she turns her head aside as the sphere dims. *Who's being childish?*

Pleasance clears the hoarse sensation, deluding a nonexistent throat. "Tell me you made them so I can forgive you again."

"I can't," he snaps, "I haven't! Don't you understand? I certainly cannot create outside our realm, I can't leave, I can't do a thing besides this! Clothes, fabric. But they're soft and useless. They disperse if—they have . . . I can't make what he—what I have always wanted to."

It couldn't be. "I heard that."

A pinhole pierces The Clouds; Pleasance squints, but she ceases when the light doesn't blind her. No, it aims into her chest.

"He's real, isn't he? The statue?"

His spherical prison allows more of the sky above to creep through. " . . . far too much to explain," he mutters, "and if she . . . "

"If I hear of this, what?"

"You'll want to sleep forever."

For her, she knows, the concept is no gentler manner of alluding to death; for she cannot die without being born, or with having no breath, no lungs; no brain to command them, nerves to numb; no bones for muscle and meat; no blood or heart. In fact the only consequences would be her freedom, and his solitude. *Does he not prefer it so?*

The Clouds lowers to the island, and he reemerges from himself as a man again, dressed in lengthy robes. Pleasance brushes a hand—while she slept, her satin body had been repaired, wrapped tighter—across the new clothing, her dress flowing and graceful as his outfit, but cinched at the waist. She has shoes; her pointed legs are pointed no longer, instead shaped around invisible feet. *I . . .* The more human she finds herself, the more she pulls away. There is a lie beneath those bandages. It is hollow, the imperceptible workings of a bodily shell.

"We can change," croons the same voice she's fluttered at since waking. Something is different.

Spite creeps across as if a colony of ants is searching for the taste on her tongue, followed surreptitiously by a cynical thought. Change is denial of their purpose—he had claimed as much previously. For cycles in years and centuries she never tallied from the start, it was he, The Clouds, who had accepted his inhumanity, acting as the foil to her love affairs of the spirit. He had refused to teach, and so she had sought a curriculum built upon dreams. Those were days she believed in their peculiar wisdom more than his profuse oppositional truths. She depended on vessels puppeteered by the psyches of man, human-thinking things, and even humans masquerading their subconscious through lucidity; she'd traversed worlds with beauty destroyed by civilizations—waterfalls, rainforests, savannas, the glaciers—; she'd fallen in love with blurry faces, desecrated them and herself, and lost every one to the inevitable opening of her eyes; she had been through Hell itself—a realm that predicates original sin; Pleasance could formulate a universe of memories, but The Clouds would play the skeptic. All the human dreams in her worlds couldn't decipher the realm of where she'd always return. Lethargy withholds her will to throw a fit; she doesn't need a nervous system to lose resolve. The Clouds put her down no matter how much she looked up in wonder. And yet, her submission now turns him on his head.

Pleasance watches the perfect sky, devoid of The Clouds. She prepares words to counter his three. Fairness and balance, just the way it should be. Their ever-wordless skyscape carefully holds her attention. *How is it blue?* She hasn't discovered the answer to that in her realm or the human worlds. *How does an island float on air and not water?* Nonsense isn't magical; it is nonsensical. *Boring.*

Her mind will be starved for truth here. *He'll change so he doesn't have the obligation to answer, he'll flatten it with some false confession.* She wants to be right about something—she never gets to be right about him.

"Pleasance, my dear, lovelorn girl." Speaking acid rain. Corrosive to the heart, but the catch is she has none. He lures again, "Please look at me."

She rebels in silence.

"There had been no manner of saving him—he didn't want to be saved."

In one glance, she forfeits.

He is pale. Not stark white as before, but a natural tone. Pinkish as blossoming carnations. Only his hair and robes are blatantly made of clouds. *And the eyes of . . .*

"Creation's gold," Pleasance says before she can stifle it; she blames his expression. His utterly pathetic look, almost mournful. Neither of them can die, nor do they deserve to harbor such a face. Humans had suffered far more—

"I've never cried. I can't harvest anything from my eyes." He smiles as if that is all he can do with confidence. "I'm ashamed of it. A cloud isn't a cloud without precipitation, but it's true, I have no rain or life—I've managed to throw lightning weaker than a pinprick. On a good day."

Pleasance is reeling.

Her response—which is to say, nothing—leaves between them the limestone, cold as she should feel, but instead, carving a burrow within, she chases herself deeper, away from the unyielding daylight; she doesn't want the sky anymore, nor him. People are driven mad when deprived of sleep and forced to endure bright places, elseways kept wide-eyed and weary by unclean thinking. Ceramics are apparently brought to fanaticism. Then collapse, eventually, when the yearning bears no fruit, and one is obligated to surrender. Pleasance cannot trace a line to the date she'd first desired to abandon ground, but it isn't worth the worry. Specifics have become pointless. She could wish and wish on the brightest stars—nightfall she'd lived through sparingly, only during sleep—while ignoring the state of her body. *Stupid, ignorant girl.* Pleasance hears The Clouds. She doesn't listen, but she takes note of the sound.

It isn't possible to hear, I haven't any real ears. In accepting herself, the senses congeal. They cease to be. After all, it's obvious: that she was, is, and forever will be a child of clay. Caught under the sun is a woman likely to crumble. And the man cradling her has no backbone.

She recovers those three words again. No use stalling—what is she afraid of?

"I—," Pleasance rasps, something eerie coughing up. Her hearing is muffled.

The Clouds strokes her bandaged shoulders with a finger.

"You . . . you make a finer human than I uphold my own name," he says.

Doughy, but not intelligible.

"But, my Pleasance, neither of us can leave this place. Our solace. It is punishment for allowing the oceans to disappear, we must endure the life sentence for an eternity."

No, you liar. She could forfeit her body and slip through dreams instead, distancing from him, until the island would become as nebulous as the minds she hops across daily, even hourly. She always could escape. The Clouds cannot interfere with the human consciousness, nor possess them. Inhabiting their bodies inhibits their sense of self, lending personality, common wisdoms, and feeling to Pleasance; should she decide to become all which rises and falls back to the Earth, she could leave The Clouds alone forever.

It was the third with golden eyes who'd told her she could—a man's voice from beyond this dimension of space. Whispers had swept into the dreamscapes, as if waterfalls could speak, and waves carried laughter.

"Ah. That's his ploy." The Clouds slides an arm behind her, supporting her back. He brings her to a sitting position, but she goes limp, avoiding the face, his facial features, where the illusion of an immutable charmer will belay her reason.

She hasn't the slightest inclination to speak.

"And yet," The Clouds begins to susurrate, "you came back to me. You share stories, adventures in other lives—if I miss a single moment, your small, sweet voice never hesitates to bring those fantasies to our reality. You always come back. Not once did you realize his offer, no matter its persistent draw of your spirit."

Pleasance flinches. She tries a murmur, though she slurs each word; her jaw is weak. "Don't have a spirit," she manages, still fumbling.

Another glance. She regrets it. His smile full of sorrows undoes the knots she'd tied around the yearning, overwhelming sensation she'd suffered wherever he went. And he is everywhere, always.

"It isn't something you have, like a name," he says with a shaking head; "it isn't so light as a word, you can't own it, nor find traces of it. You *are* your spirit—you are you."

The twitching bandaged hands. His cheek is there, very close, very much within reach. To hold his face would let him win. Pleasance relaxes her limbs in opposition, but the itch—not just on the surface; it's deeper, an appetite for *something real*—begs her fingertips to agree. *He looks . . . he can't be human, he can't.* She peruses the outline from his chin to the clouds blossoming above and around him. *We are not humans.* Pleasance finally understands.

She finds no heartbeat at his center. "We don't have one."

"Hearts?" he says. "Perhaps not."

"You were right."

"I know, but I wish you wouldn't sound so dreary."

She wonders if he'll look somewhere else soon.

"Pleasance?"

His golds reflect a startled expression of hers.

"I have . . . I imagined you would leave if I answered your question," says The Clouds, "and in hiding the truth, the irony of it is that I only drove you away further. 'What is enticing about the dreams? What do *I* lack?' I'd think each time you closed your eyes. My creation is no talent—clouds are weak fabrics, you see. But I was born to watch over. Perception is my greatest gift.

"The moment your eyelids succumb to exhaustion and stress, our world mirrors it. Gateways burst open to the north, poking holes into your unconscious journeys and the sky alike, where I'm left to peer through their windows, which aren't much windows at all, and well, they are *doors,* and I've passed thresholds to join you in sleep. Because I can't. I don't really feel tired or hungry or thirsty, unlike you. How much did you suffer? Senses that cannot be sated, physical limitations . . . I couldn't bear it.

"Humans dream too much. Whether they remember or not, you've been unable to forget them." He leans in, taking to her ear. "It is an unequivocal disdain I have for the human race who tempts you, teaches you things, pollutes your mind with ideas of *spirit* as if they're the only creatures who have them. It isn't right. It isn't fair to you. Blood or no, hearts or hardened clay, what matters is your self. We both have a self. We have spirits and metaphorical hearts. *They* don't even realize you're there."

As thinking gradually loses its bitterness, Pleasance indulges it. Lauds his roundabout sermon, first; though the wrappings conceal her mouth, she suspects he won't miss the displacement brought upon by her wide grin. Second, and most importantly, she stops herself before she grabs his robes. Restraint. Careful, painful restraint.

The Clouds belongs within, holding her body together. Such soft arms; he must be straining to keep himself touchable. For her sake.

"Pleasance"—*oh,* but it's agonizing to hear her name!—"you hadn't inquired this, but—difficult as it is, I—I can't tell you unless you promise you'll . . . no, no, it doesn't have to be that. Please promise me you'll give warning, if you must go. Don't vanish."

When his voice lulls, the world lightens—in weight, not color; as a matter of fact, the hues fade and age before Pleasance notices, and so the shift appears to flicker from vibrant, satiating aquas, leafy greens, and milky whites, to the darkened, retching splatters surrounding their island center, skies rolling gray as the storms she'd witnessed in slumber.

"There are stronger vows I'd make for you," Pleasance entrusts naturally, not a word thought out. "I don't want to waste time on those that don't matter."

"It matters to me," he says.

She . . . she hadn't considered him for once.

"Perhaps I do hear your mind at rest, or when it starts to churn, but there is no intent I can glean from those feelings. In the end, I've had to make assumptions as much as you do."

But had he not been correct about her so far? Even she relents as much.

The Clouds shakes his head once; his loitering pair of eyes he keeps attentive to the grass, not her, as their world bathes them in cold; the overcast layer needs no consideration from them for its intrusion to persist.

Pleasance flexes her fingers. "Explain."

"Promise," he says, "and I'll illuminate everything you've asked."

Her hand fights with the recently tightened bandages, removing them from the top, the tip of a molded nose, and she places the satin strands on her collar; and as she regards the fullness to his face, restraint becomes an absurdity. Those falsehoods she'd dreamt were pyrite compared to his handsome rose gold, even if he could never shed a tear. Creation is not reserved for definite objects. Despite her devotion to The Clouds, Pleasance hadn't thanked him—she had demanded, but rarely reciprocated; to think he'd sired the prayer for a heart! That should have been worth all the more affection than she could carry. As he carries her in his lap.

She pecks his cheek.

The Clouds exclaims a non-word, then her name, and turns his cheek aside as if to ward off confusion or excitement. But he's exposed his neck. Just above the nape of it, his clouded hair blusters eastward.

"I only asked—," he tries.

Her lips plant a swift one under his ear.

"Pleasance!" he cries.

"I promise," she answers, "I will leave only if there's nothing for me here."

Faltering, he doesn't return her look too suddenly, the sort of motion done to keep from scaring an idle finch. To watch without confronting.

"Very well." The Clouds tucks a finger under a bandage, a slackened ribbon at her shoulder. He smiles. "Then I suppose I'll have to give you everything, if I'm to attain what I need."

Better to guess instead of letting him speak hazily. "To live alone unconditionally?" she asks.

"You."

Warmth radiates up to her head—scalds as his fog surrounds them, hissing steam.

The finger he'd woven through the wrapping is followed by the next on his hand, then the other, and the rest, each tugging her satin body loose.

Her clothing—made from The Clouds—now bursts and rushes to him, baring the remaining bandages around her torso. Gnawing a piece at her neck, he takes it firmly between his teeth and rips it free. More of her unravels. Pleasance closes an eye, curious vision of the other studying his movement. His gliding hands untying her body, with a sleeve of his robe falling halfway down his shoulder. A smirk when he catches her gandering.

Pleasance flinches at the sight—a body, ceramic as her skull. Where the sculptural bust had been is a smooth, somewhat budding chest, the subtle indication of a ribcage. The Clouds rends off her wrappings in a descent, revealing yet another gray portion of a figure—*her* figure, not air. A waist, navel, and hips; he lingers at her right, pressing his reddening face to a bandaged thigh.

"Heavens, I don't need to go *this* far," he mutters in argument with himself. It can't be directed at her. She hasn't stopped him.

Pleasance settles into the thick cloud propping her up. Though she lifts an arm, perhaps to comfort or encourage him, she notices that even her hands are formed. She admires the palm, the detail to ceramic phalanges. *Had he crafted this body?* The fingers bend like organic things, disobeying the laws of pottery. Laughable—she shouldn't be so perplexed. After all, her head defies the material, as well.

"We aren't bound to whatever human worlds observe, Pleasance," says The Clouds, a bashful, lowered cadence to him. He sidles up again, crawling above her chest. Leaving the bandages to emulate a pair of tights. His cheek nestles into her collar. "Here, if a cloud can become a person, why not a statue?"

Statue . . . The Clouds has once again encased her in a cushioned sanctuary, albeit with his human mimicry to accompany her, unlike before. Upon a moment's inspection, she finds she cannot see the pedestals through the billowing white. But they must be there—she'd memorized the direction. North.

"You . . . you said you'd give me an answer," utters Pleasance, staring, "after I made the promise."

"So I did," says The Clouds.

"Don't renege."

"I'm not."

"You're distracting me, like you always do," she fusses.

"Because it riles your heart and brings me pleasure." He taps a finger at the center of her chest. Somehow, when he drags a line across, it dips in at the exact midpoint. "That is why."

Pretending she'd heard nothing, Pleasance copies him, searching the spot with hesitant fingertips. She stops. There is a pinhole in her chest.

"What is this?" She prods it, covers it, uncovers it. "Shouldn't I be complete? Why did you leave a hole?" Furthermore, she pokes the center for emphasis. "And why *here* of all places?"

"You are baked clay," he says flatly, "I would have thought you understood. . . . And because—where else did you think I would . . . ?"

Pleasance ceases her squirming. If only it were possible to take back ignorant questions.

The Clouds, as expected, slowly shakes his head. "I suppose I should demonstrate."

No you don't! She grabs his hand as he starts. "Answer, first. About the statues. About him, the other one."

Their comforting cocoon darkens to a gray once more. The Clouds swallows, his eyes aglow and glancing off.

"I've said it," he mumbles, "that he didn't want saving."

"Everything. I'll take all the story you're able to tell."

Sorrow seems to afflict The Clouds. "Then, had you known there was never another head?"

But there are two busts, two pedestals. If her head had tumbled off, by consequence of too thin a neck, the second sculpture must have been the same. Otherwise, how ridiculous! *Why would anyone—?*

"Art, Pleasance, often means more than its artist is willing to admit. In his case, he told me what you were, and I—I surveyed the process, his careful hand, the clay he dug from the island and manipulated until he brought you into our world. The statues were his manner of expression."

"A headless bust! And I was—"

"You stood for thoughtfulness, brooding. *Pleasance Triste.*"

She hates her second name. "Don't remind me of it."

"It was no accident you chose two names for yourself. The title is one he bestowed on his finished work, the pair of unpainted ceramic busts."

"I swear I misspoke—," Pleasance stammers. "You told me I couldn't take back naming myself twice!"

"So I did." He lowers his head, folding half his body over her. "So I did."

By every measure, she should be in an angrier place, but somehow, the effort for such negativity has less appeal than it had in the past.

"You really are an airbrain," she grumbles.

"To say nothing of you," he remarks quite discreetly, though not silent enough. His hand falls upon her chest again.

Pleasance prods his knuckles. "I hate you."

The Clouds purrs.

"Answer my damned question."

"Yes, yes," he says quickly, "I was getting to it." He sighs. "I was . . . getting there, talking of him. Of *Pleasance Triste*"—she chews her lip as he continues—"the *magnum opus* he entrusted me. I'm your caretaker, or I suppose I once was."

Recalling the older memories is as smooth as sandpaper, and it does shave away the more Pleasance strains to retrace those first steps. Herself, an adult, with an unassuming woman's features. Someone held Pleasance above calm waters, where she could greet her own reflection. *I'd spoken to myself.* Embarrassing—that is precisely it. She *had* said "hello" to the face staring at her mysteriously, as if this woman meant to mock her.

The Clouds strokes his thumb over the hole in her chest. "He was there during the years of your formative mind. He didn't trust me to educate you on things besides what you instinctively knew."

The back of his hand is soft, too. Natural. Pleasance touches considerately.

"*Orders*. No less esoteric a name as his reasoning behind yours—you, as in, the work itself. Orders emerged from the ocean of his body and set foot on the grass ages ago. Long before you. When sand outlined the shore, and our island was larger, he arrived as some figure of a man. Liquid structure in a solid silhouette. I hadn't spoken a word before, but I shouted at him, 'Someone is here!' I was elated.

"I thought nobody could speak or hear the way I did, until Orders searched for the source of my voice. 'Someone *is* here,' he said a bit differently, all the urgency of a philosopher lost in a haunted cave. Stated so plain and insightful. Contrary to my overt eagerness, Orders was not amused by a greeting from the sky.

"'What a bother,' he confided in the grass, 'I won't be able to focus.' Imagine that! He was asking to be pestered, honestly. Forever passed as I did just as I wanted, rambling, sending gusts through his watery body, watching him pace around the center. He always stepped between it and the cardinal markers—he avoided the stones as if they were diseased. Only a fateful day did he finally look up and respond in kind. Yes, he had ignored me until then. Maybe I should have shut up once he'd spoken to me directly.

"But can you guess this wonderful day? It should be easy," The Clouds warbles.

Pleasance snaps out of her listening trance. "Uhm, I suppose," she says, "you mean the day I awoke."

He hugs closer. "Ah, of course, I knew you would understand—it couldn't have been anything else." A tiny inhale of his breathes out in a huff. "If only a calendar could mark our days! Too many, Pleasance. It has been a long, long time since I met you."

"Yes, but about him—Orders, that one. I have no recollection, but I feel I should, a little." The chubbiness to his face sinks into the sturdy, buffed sculpt of her own cheek. "I don't. It's unusual."

"He had not been concerned with your knowing of him, no. I—*he* said, I believe, 'Can you guard her when she wakes? I am going somewhere.' He gave me enough time for a 'yes, but—' and 'excuse me!'

before gathering the waters, balling them, and holding them in his hand. An ocean in the palm of his hand!"

"Impossible as a flying island."

The Clouds does grin again, if the slight shift in his jaw is any indication. Could be half-willed. "I meant it was a portent for his talent, admirable strength of an even stronger mind. We live in the opposite of impossibility, limited only by our imaginations and spiritual fortitude. Thus . . . we may be closer to the primordial universe, according to him. Humans are the inferior progeny. They abide by laws and propagate in droves, perfecting nothing—those who nearly reach enlightenment cannot survive beyond mortality, either."

"Breakable things are more valuable, as dying things find a greater respect for life."

"Similarly, quantity diminishes the value of things, brittle or not."

"We are rounding this topic too frequently as of late," says Pleasance. "More people means more stories, more for *us* to enjoy—how does a populated world erode life's extraordinary complexity? By definition, it adds to the beauty. It doesn't ruin it."

"Pleasance, your ability to gape through those doors would *not* have existed on their law-driven planet. If you were human, your eyes would commit to the most immediate elements of your life, you'd never see the world honestly, from afar, not even a feigned compassion could reflect the manner in which you treat them—humanity—with liberal, impartial consideration. To contain their ambitions, humans are crippled by nature and civilization alike. Orders knew this. He knew he'd never be able to return if he reshaped himself, but he left and spread his body across many Earths."

"What! You remember him so easily and throw this upon me now?"

"If I had told you that Orders cannot reverse his choice, would you have stayed?"

Pleasance thinks, but turns up blank.

"No. You might have thought to test my presumed lie before crushing yourself into pieces and sprinkling the remains onto mountains, deserts, canyons, plains—anywhere." Despite the words chiseling at her heart, his voice is relaxed and somewhat exhausted, crackling as the impassioned volume peaks at a murmur. "I would never forgive myself if you had forfeited your body just to partake in human rituals."

Perhaps that revelation is too thick for The Clouds' nonchalant portrayal; why would he withhold everything from her just to protect her? Orders has no power over him. Orders surrendered to the law-abiding Earth.

Hanging by the concept of self—she was an artwork, she was *created*—and sinking into the musing tides, Pleasance inhales sluggishly, imagining a diaphragm where one can never exist. Unchallenged truth didn't hurt as *this* had gripped her. She had quarreled against inhumanity until she would lose her voice yelling, but now, opposing it was this clay fool's errand. She wasn't human. She'd never be human.

"Orders sculpted you from his body and the island's clay—he is connected to you, through lingering moisture, but I am exiled to your surface."

It hits Pleasance harder. Today she finally learned of the creator; she *has* one. But if she does, it disagrees with The Clouds and his insistence on their realm having no coherence. Couldn't a nonsense place have a sculpture with no artist? It could. It should have could—Pleasance refocuses her eyes along with the unruly vocabulary.

Proof, that's what I need. The Clouds claims she was once inanimate, but had no evidence. *Does he?* Would he lie? He kept Pleasance unaware, and she let him. Whispers sung on the threaded breeze. But would he invent a false person to keep her? Orders wasn't much of a name—then again, neither was Pleasance or The Clouds or Triste—and men didn't come from the ocean—nor were they made of evaporated water, steam, thunder, static—and, and, their world did not follow a single thing properly. To which standard? Humans, the people from dreams. *Humans.* They could have been tenuous, unreal concepts too.

" . . . I'm a passing idea—Orders even persists within me."

Logic plucks and draws a wire of some association, pulling from her findings; indeed, water cycles around the seas, rivers, skies, and it perpetuates. *Orders.* The ocean, was he not? An anomaly would have been The Clouds—who doesn't rain—appearing with the inception of their realm.

"Because clouds are made from oceans," Pleasance finishes. *Or, I wonder, would it be more appropriate if he had been the eldest?*

There is some pause, then the steam dissolves above her, only to roll over in a silkier mist.

"I—maybe true of Earths, but I," says The Clouds, filling uncertainty with hums, "am older than Orders, but younger than our ocean."

"An ocean made you both, then, same as an Earth law."

"So—?"

"So the humans are real somewhere, and we share universal truths. Obviously."

"Now *you're* circling a subject," The Clouds jabs.

They live nowhere and always go nowhere. "I'm tired of listening," Pleasance submits, "and I'm to blame for asking."

Stroking the long, clumped strands of gold, glittering clay—her hair—The Clouds combs his fingertips down, lifting them to start from her parted hairline once again.

"That is the inevitability of the *Triste*," he says with a pat to the spot he'd straightened. "Erm, it could very well be a poor interpretation, since Orders hadn't elaborated, but I find his work speaks for itself."

Sculptures, fakes. Soulless.

"I suppose you missed the pun."

Humor is a league unto its own, and not even mortal life could define it. Amusing as a joke can be to one person, another may find it bland, at worst despicable. *Art must be similar,* she imagines. *Ah, but I'm the piece of work. I shouldn't have an opinion about myself.*

"See?" The Clouds pokes her in the temple. "Your head fell off because it overflowed, Pleasance."

There are enough realities for a dreadful amount of self-absorption. Abyssal gazing had inspired her once, but it ate her on the inside; details don't cease to multiply. People can eventually cause themselves a genetic bottleneck, while ideas grow faster than splitting, festering bacteria.

Again The Clouds delights in touching her playfully—shoulder prodding, kneading an arm, accosting the waist—but a statue cannot be tickled, of course. The dearth of even a shudder must bewilder him. He allows his hand to brush aslant, and down, to limply settle at her bandaged thigh.

"The *Pleasance* is a spirit without a head, blissful, lacking thoughts and capacity for action," he carefully utters. "*Triste* has a skull, a visage, along with every sense to collect information from the world: ears, attuned to vibrations; eyes, preoccupied with the colors and movements of the living; a nose, underappreciated for its early warnings; feeling skin, unlike the numb, headless half; and the mouth, having taste on its discreet tongue. And she thinks and wonders and ponders and laments for years, cursed by comprehension, or perhaps by awareness seeking comprehension, a hunger that will never be sated so long as concepts expand with the universe in tandem with people arguing sides that reject a middle ground. *Pleasance* cares not for these inconsequential details. She has no head and sense to cultivate concerns."

His speech brings about a thought—an insult. Pleasance blinks as it creeps up, luring the divergent idea, but she snatches its snoutful front and clamps the thing shut. None will hear. If she halts before The Clouds shares her thinking, then neither are required to address it in any possible way.

"*Pleasance,* who has no ability to know, remains blissful—and beside her, *Triste* succumbs as stimulation drags her head from the neck, casting her to the depths of listless futility. Unsatisfied because she always wants. *Pleasance Triste* is both at once—you are never obligated to study eternally," The Clouds says, his forearm beginning to fidget. "I hope you don't."

"Orders regrets it, I think," he mumbles, "that he left you in my care. I paid him back by ignoring *him* and the constant pestering. Ever since he bled into waters across the Earths . . . ever since, as well, his transcendence of time, space, and matter . . . I like to pretend he's jealous of us. We enjoy the life he'd abandoned."

"Pleasance," his ramble persists, "remember the echoes we both endured for those early days? They weren't your dreams—I lied there, yes. Again. It occurs without my planning, you see.

"Orders was a more impulsive man. Opinionated, as well, very very opinionated. Angry at humanity. I may agree on principle, but he lost the moment he departed. I have to laugh at him a little.

"'What gives them the right to dictate we came second? Or that we were never here in the first place?'

"'Had we sprung from chaos before humanity?'

"'I'll show them. I'll give up my purpose for an answer.'

"Answer? An answer to what? After that, would he be happy?"

Pleasance giggles lightly from the chest, feeling its rumble through her throat. "No, of course he wouldn't."

With a sharp, triumphant sigh, The Clouds buries into his own pillowy bed; so does Pleasance, suddenly thankful she isn't against the center limestone. Had they remained grounded, or had The Clouds floated into the air while they were speaking? *Does it matter?* She squints, fascinated with his gathering woolen hair, rays of light poking through and disappearing as unpredictably as any weather.

That troublemaker is blither-blathering where Pleasance understands her jawline meets a newly fortified neck. *Thanks to him.*

"You owe . . . more stories . . . *issonly fair* . . . ." The Clouds gulps, breaking into a yawn.

Pleasance catches it.

Stars flicker at the back of her mind. An evening lulls into a restful paradise, cooling beneath a roving vessel's skin. Forming her unconscious attachment, she dreams of holding up her wrist, extracting a golden pen from an eye, a blank tome falling at her lap. But she isn't asleep today. Somehow the realms intertwine, and a trance immerses her curious girl in the task. In a glance, Pleasance finds the man still draped over her body. His hair, thinner than smoke, glides noiselessly through the pinhole in her chest. The Clouds had drifted off.

It may break her, but she will not change.

As long as Prima shone down, she would not end.

"I must be who I am and never what I want."

She walked in search of him again.

"I am alone."